Cameron couldn't breathe, couldn't think, couldn't form a damn thought with Megan's curvy body pressed against his.

This was his best friend, yet with the way she was all but spilling out of her barely there black dress, his thoughts weren't very friend-like at the moment.

Hadn't he just pep-talked himself into trying to keep his thoughts out of the gutter?

"Wh-what are you doing here?" she asked.

Why was her voice all breathy and sultry?

Cameron dropped his hands, took a step back, but that didn't help his hormones settle down. Now he was able to see just how hot she looked wearing that second-skin dress that hit her upper thigh at a very indecent level.

Jealousy ripped through him. "Where the hell are you going like that?"

THE ST. JOHNS OF STONEROCK:
Three rebellious brothers come home to stay

Dear Reader,

I hope you've enjoyed the intriguing St. John brothers as much as I have. You've met Eli (*Dr. Daddy's Perfect Christmas*) and Drake (*The Fireman's Ready-Made Family*); now it's time for Cameron to get his story, and he's just as demanding and powerful as the others. This hardworking, mysterious brother isn't going to fall in love with just anyone...he's falling hard and fast for his best friend.

I admit, best friends falling in love is one of my favorite tropes. The connection and chemistry is already there just waiting to cross into passion and love. Megan has loved Cam for years, but she's afraid to risk their solid friendship, and he's never given her a sign he's interested in her "that way." What's a girl to do?

I love how Cameron is this great big protector where Megan is concerned. He's halfway in love with her, but vows to put her needs ahead of his own...a true hero. Circumstances change for both of them and each seeks comfort in the other. Outside forces push them together, really pulling out their inner emotions. Even with Cam's secrets to protect Megan, she knows he loves her...now if she could just get him to admit it.

Cam will risk it all for the woman he loves. His career and his family have always been top priority in his life, but he soon finds out his world is empty without his best friend by his side—permanently.

Sit back and enjoy this last installment of my St. John brothers and watch as Cam finds himself venturing into territory he'd sworn off...love.

Happy reading!

Jules Bennett

From Best Friend
to Bride

—

Jules Bennett

HARLEQUIN® SPECIAL EDITION®

Recycling programs
for this product may
not exist in your area.

ISBN-13: 978-0-373-65887-9

From Best Friend to Bride

Copyright © 2015 by Jules Bennett

Printed in U.S.A.

Award-winning author **Jules Bennett** is no stranger to romance—she met her husband when she was only fourteen. After dating through high school, the two married. He encouraged her to chase her dream of becoming an author. Jules has now published nearly thirty novels. She and her husband are living their own happily-ever-after while raising two girls. Jules loves to hear from readers through her website, julesbennett.com, her Facebook fan page or on Twitter.

Books by Jules Bennett

Harlequin Special Edition

The St. Johns of Stonerock

The Fireman's Ready-Made Family
Dr. Daddy's Perfect Christmas

Harlequin Desire

The Barrington Trilogy

When Opposites Attract...
Single Man Meets Single Mom
Carrying the Lost Heir's Child

Visit the Author Profile page at Harlequin.com for more titles.

There's nothing like spending all of your days with your best friend. This book is dedicated to not only my best friend, but my real-life hero. Love you, Michael, and I love our very own happily ever after.

Chapter One

"You know how to please a man."

Megan Richards desperately wished those words coming from her best friend's kissable lips had been said in a different context. Alas, Cameron St. John was only referring to the medium-well steak she had grilled, and not a bedroom romp.

One day she would shock them both when she declared her desire, her need for the man she'd known since kindergarten, when he'd pulled her pigtails and she'd retaliated by taking her safety scissors to his mullet. A mutual respect was instantly born, and they'd been friends since—sans pigtails and mullet.

"I figured you'd been eating enough take-out junk and needed some real food," she told him, watching in admiration as he picked up their dinner plates and started loading her dishwasher.

Oh, yeah. His mama had raised him right, and Megan didn't think there was a sexier sight than a domestic man…especially one with muscles that flexed so beautifully with each movement.

Since his back was turned, she soaked up the view. The man came by his rippled beauty honestly, with hours dedicated to rigorous workouts. She worked out, too—just last night she'd exercised with a box of cookies—which would be the main reason his body was so perfectly toned while hers was so perfectly dimpled and shapely.

Cameron closed the dishwasher door and gave the countertop a swift swipe with the cloth before turning to face her. With his hands resting on either side of his narrow hips, he might have looked all laid-back and casual, but the man positively reeked of alpha sexiness. His impressive height and broad shoulders never failed to send a sucker punch straight to her active hormones.

Too bad he was married to his job as chief of police in Stonerock, Tennessee. Besides, she was too afraid to lose him as a friend to really open up and let years of emotions come pouring out. Well, that and Cameron and his family had been the only true stability she'd known since her parents were killed in a car accident during a snowstorm when they'd been traveling up north to visit friends. Megan couldn't risk damaging the bond she had with Cam.

Oh, and he'd made it perfectly clear on more than one occasion that he wouldn't get into a committed relationship. Not as long as he was in law enforcement, thanks to an incident involving his partner when they'd been rookies.

Yup, he didn't do relationships; just like he didn't do healthy food.

"I don't eat junk," he defended himself.

Megan tipped her head, quirking a brow.

"I'll have you know that Burger-rama is real food, and they know my order without me even repeating it." Cameron crossed his arms over his wide chest and offered her that lady-killer smile.

Laughing, Megan came to her feet. "I rest my case."

With a quick glance at his watch, Cameron pushed off the counter and sighed. "I better get going. I need to rest before heading out tonight."

She had no clue what he was working on; she rarely did. He was pretty adamant about keeping his work absent from their conversations. He'd tell the occasional funny drunken-fight story, but when it came to a serious investigative case, he was pretty tight-lipped.

Whatever he was working on must be major, seeing as how he'd been heading out to work at midnight several nights a week—not something a chief normally did. The new lines between his brows and the dark circles beneath his eyes spoke volumes about his new schedule.

"You're working yourself to death. You know that, right? Between all the crazy hours and the junk food. You can't be getting enough sleep."

One corner of his mouth tipped up in a smile. That cocky, charming grin always had the same heart-

gripping impact. How many women had been mes-
merized by that beautiful, sexy smile?

"I'll be fine," he assured her, pulling her into a
friendly hug. "This case should wrap up soon, and
I'll be back to somewhat normal hours, complete with
sleep. The junk food remains, though."

Two out of three wasn't too bad. Besides, normal for
him meant ten-hour days instead of twelve or fourteen.
Reminding him of his father's bypass surgery last year
would do no good. The St. John men were a stubborn
bunch. She should know; she'd been the family side-
kick since grade school.

Megan kept her mouth shut and wrapped her arms
around his waist as she slowly inhaled his familiar
scent. Closing her eyes, she wished for so much. She
wished Cam would wake up and see how deeply she
cared for him, she wished her brother would straighten
his life out and she wished she knew what to do about
the out-of-town job offer she'd just received.

None of those things were going to happen right
now, so she held on tight and enjoyed the moment of
being enveloped by the man she'd loved for years. If
friendship was all they were destined for, then she'd
treasure what she had and not dwell on the unattain-
able.

Cameron eased back, resting his firm hands on her
shoulders. "You okay? You seem tense."

Really? Because she'd pretty much melted into his
embrace. The cop in him always managed to pick up
every little detail around him, yet the man in him was
totally oblivious to the vibes she sent out. It would be

so much easier if he just magically knew how she felt and took that giant first step so she didn't have to. The passive-aggressive thing was never her style, but in this instance she really wished he'd just read her mind.

"I'm fine," she assured him, offering a grin. "Just a lot on my mind lately."

Wasn't that an understatement?

His dark brows drew together as those signature bright blue St. John eyes studied her. "What can I do to help?"

Oh, if he only knew. One day.

"Nothing." She reached up, patted his stubbled jaw and stepped back to avoid further temptation. "Go rest so you can head out and save Stonerock from all the bad guys."

The muscle in his jaw jumped. "I'm working on it."

"I hope you're careful," she added, always worried she'd get a phone call from one of his brothers or his parents telling her the worst. Because Cameron would put his life on the line for anybody. He just wouldn't put his heart on the line.

He laughed. "Yes, Mom, I'm careful."

Swatting him on his hard pec, Megan narrowed her eyes. "I have to ask. You make me worry."

"Nothing to worry about," he assured her, with a friendly kiss on her forehead. "I'm good at my job."

"You're so humble, too."

With a shrug, he pulled his keys from his pocket. "Eli and Nora's baby is being christened tomorrow. You're still planning on coming, right?"

"Are you going to make it?"

Cameron nodded and headed toward the back door. He always came and went via her back door. He never knocked, just used a key when it was locked and made himself at home.

"I'll make it," he told her, his hand resting on the antique knob. "I may even have time to run home and nap and shower for the occasion."

"How about I pick you up?" she offered.

He lived in her neighborhood, and they tended to ride together when they went anywhere. They were pretty much like an old married couple, you know, just without the sex and shared living quarters.

"Be there at nine." His finger tapped on the door-knob. "Lock up behind me."

Rolling her eyes, she gave him a mock salute as he left. The worry was definitely a two-way street.

Now that she was alone with her thoughts, she had to face the unknowns that circled around in her mind. This job offer had come out of nowhere.

Was it a sign that she needed to move on? She'd been in Stonerock nearly her entire life; she was still single and had nothing holding her back.

Except Cameron.

After scrubbing her sink and table, Megan was still no closer to making a decision. She loved being a therapist at the local counseling center; she loved her patients and truly felt as if she was making an impact in their lives.

The new job would be in Memphis, nearly two hours away. The new facility would offer her a chance at helping more people, even taking charity cases, which would allow her to comfort and guide people she never could've reached otherwise.

How could she say no?

As she sank onto the chair at her kitchen table, she thought of her brother. He was an adult, but he'd never been able to take care of himself. The questionable decisions he made kept snowballing into more bad decisions—each one seemingly worse than the last. He always counted on her as a crutch to fall back on. What would happen to him if she left? Would he finally man up and take control of his life? See just how dependent he'd become and actually want to change?

More to the point: What would happen with Cameron? Before she made the decision, she would have to seriously consider gathering up the courage to tell him the secret she kept in the pit of her soul.

This job was a catalyst for pushing her in that direction. She needed to move on one way or another… though she'd rather move on with him. Either way, she'd know if years of wanting and dreaming had been for naught.

She'd wanted a relationship with him since they'd graduated high school, but the timing to reveal her feelings had never been right. Between her parents' deaths, his deployment and Megan always putting her life on hold to help her brother, she just had never found an opening.

Cameron was the only solid foundation in her life. What happened if she told him how much she loved him and it ruined their friendship? Could she take that risk?

He'd told her he'd never consider being in a committed relationship. He'd shared the story of the night his partner had died and how he'd had to witness the widow's complete breakdown. Cam had told her he'd never put anyone through that.

Still, she had to let him know how she felt. She couldn't go through life playing the what-if game forever, and he deserved to know. By not giving him a chance to make a decision, she could be missing out on the best thing that had ever happened to her.

Megan folded her arms across the table and rested her head on them. She really had no choice...not if she wanted to live her life without regrets.

Some risks were worth taking. She knew without a doubt if Cameron wanted to take things beyond friendship, the joy would be totally worth the bundle of nerves that had taken up residence in her stomach.

Cameron had managed about a three-hour nap before the christening. He'd also showered and shaved for the occasion. His mother would be so proud.

He'd just finished adjusting his navy tie when his front door opened and closed. Heels clicked on the hardwood floor, growing louder as Megan approached the hallway. He assumed the visitor was Megan, unless one of his brothers had opted to don stilettos today.

He knew of Megan's love for breakneck shoes when she wasn't wearing her cowgirl boots. Didn't matter to him if she was barefoot. Cameron had fought his attraction to Megan for a few years now. At first he'd thought the temptation would go away. No such luck. Being a cop's wife, even in a small town, wasn't something he'd put on anyone he cared about. He couldn't handle knowing he'd put the worry and stress of being a cop's wife on Megan, so he pulled up every bit of his self-control to block his true feelings.

Unfortunately, Cameron had never wanted to avoid his best friend as much as he did right this moment. Dread filled his stomach as he recalled the things he'd witnessed last night while monitoring the drugstore parking lot. The events that had unfolded on his watch put a whole new spin on this case…and quite possibly his relationship with Megan. No, not quite possibly. Without a doubt the new developments would shatter their perfect bond.

Her brother had gotten involved with the wrong crowd—a crowd Cameron was about to take down.

She deserved to be happy, deserved to live free from her brother's illegal activities, and Cameron would do anything and everything to keep Megan safe.

Although he was torn about whether or not she should find out, he was obligated to his job first, which meant he had to keep every bit of this operation to himself. She would be hurt and angry when she discovered what her brother was doing, and even more so when she realized Cameron had hidden the truth from her.

"You wearing pants?" she called out.

With a chuckle, Cameron shoved his wallet and phone into his back pocket. "Pants are a requirement?"

When he stepped into the hall, he stopped short. *Damn.* Megan had always been beautiful, and she always presented herself as classy and polished for work, but this morning she looked even more amazing than usual. There went that twist to his heart, the one that confirmed she was the most perfect woman for him. But he couldn't let her in, wouldn't subject her to his chaotic schedule, his stress from the job. Because if he was stressed, he knew she'd want to take some on herself to relieve him of any burden. He'd signed up for this career…Megan hadn't.

With her fitted red dress, a slim black belt accentuating her small waist and rounded hips and her dark hair down around her shoulders, she stole his breath— something that rarely happened with any woman. Always Megan. Everything was always centered around Megan. She was special.

Which was why he shouldn't be looking at her as if she were a woman he'd met at a bar and wanted to bring home for the night. Not that he remembered what that was like. He hadn't been in a bar for personal recreation in so long, never mind bringing a woman back to his bed.

Megan deserved to be treasured, to be loved and come first in any man's life. Unfortunately he could only offer two of the three.

Cameron had always figured one of his brothers would scoop Megan up, and the thought had crippled him each time the image crept through his mind. Thankfully, both Eli and Drake had found the loves of their lives. Cameron was thrilled for them, but love wasn't for all the St. John boys. Cameron barely had time to catch any sleep, let alone devote to a relationship.

"Should I go back home and change?" she asked,

raising a brow with a smirk on her face. "You're staring at me."

"No, no." He adjusted his jacket, hating the confining garment and feeling somewhat naked without his shoulder holster. "You're just looking exceptionally beautiful this morning."

"You mean my old paint-stained tank and tattered shorts I had on yesterday didn't make me look beautiful?" She fluttered her eyelids in a mocking manner he found ridiculously attractive.

He loved that no matter what life threw at her, she always found a way to be a bit snarky. Why hadn't some guy come along and swept her off her feet? Any man would be lucky to have her. She grilled an amazing steak, she was always there for him no matter what, she joked and she even drank beer with him.

If she married someone who loved her and treated her the way she deserved to be treated, Cameron might be able to get this notion that he was worthy of her out of his head. Because he sure as hell knew that was false. He wanted to see her happy with that family she'd always wanted. But she wasn't even dating anybody. Still, he couldn't tell her his feelings because there wasn't a happy ending if he chose that path. Telling Megan would only cause an awkward, uncomfortable wedge between them, and hurting her in any way would destroy him.

As she stood in his hallway, looking like a classy pinup model with all her curves, Cameron cursed himself for allowing his thoughts to travel where they had no business going. Her curves weren't new, but when the two of them got together she never dressed like this.

It was the dress. That perfectly molded dress. He was used to seeing her in professional work clothes or old tees and shorts. If he was looking at her in a way that stirred him, how would other men be looking at her today? They were attending a church service, for crying out loud, and he was standing here fighting off an ever-growing attraction to his best friend. There was so much wrong with this situation he didn't even know where to start.

"I'm ready." He moved into the foyer, careful not to touch her as he passed, and retrieved his keys from the side table.

After he'd locked up behind them, Cameron followed her down the stone path toward her black SUV parked in his drive. They'd barely gotten their seat belts fastened before her cell chimed. Casting a quick glance down to where it rested on the console, Cameron spotted Evan's name on the screen. More anxiety filled his stomach, but he kept his mouth shut. Now was not the time to expose him. He'd actually made a point to not come between Megan and her brother. Their issues went way beyond those of regular siblings. He might not be able to tell Megan what had happened last night, but Cameron would throw himself in front of her to protect her from anyone…including Evan. Family loyalty meant everything to him; unfortunately, her brother was only loyal to himself.

Megan's bright green eyes darted up to his as she sighed. "I'm sorry."

Wasn't that the story of her life? Always apologizing for her brother, always coming to his defense? Megan was never fully able to live her own life the way she wanted because she'd had to play mom, dad, sister and therapist to the ungrateful punk for years.

She snatched her cell on the second ring. "Hello."

Cameron couldn't make out what Evan was saying, only the rumble of a male voice filtered through the SUV. Not that Cameron needed to know what Evan was saying. The man only called his sister to ask for money, use her car or some other random favor.

Megan's head fell against the back of her seat as she gripped the phone with one hand and her steering wheel with the other. "I can't, Evan—I'm busy right now."

Cameron resisted the urge to pull the phone from her hand and tell Evan to grow a set and quit using his sister as plan A. The man, and he used the term loosely, had never held a job that Cameron was aware of…or at least not a legal one. Evan had been a troublemaker in school, getting kicked out of two before he even started junior high. Megan's parents had moved the family to the next town as a result of Evan's troubles, causing Cameron and Megan to lose touch for a year. Thankfully Megan had transferred back and their relationship had picked up right where they'd left off—with them goofing off and her hanging at his house with him and his brothers.

Unfortunately, switching schools had only made Evan angrier, resulting in his behavior growing more reckless. Now, as an adult, he had made no strides to clean himself up. Actually, after what Cameron had witnessed last night, he knew Evan was even worse than he'd thought. The man was straight up running drugs. And there was no way in hell Megan knew the trouble her brother was in.

No wonder Megan adored Cameron's family so much. They were all she had in the form of a loving, solid foundation.

"I'm sorry, Evan," she went on, her tone exhausted. "That's not something I can do right now. If you can wait until this afternoon, then I can help. Otherwise, I don't know what to tell you."

The more Megan argued, defending herself, the more Cameron felt his blood pressure soar. He was thankful that even though he and his brothers had been hellions in school, they'd never crossed the line into illegal activity. They'd been standard cocky teens. There just happened to be three of them with that arrogant attitude, and when one had done something, the others had jumped on board.

"No, Evan, I—"

Cameron refused to let this go on another second. He pried the phone from her hand and ended the call without a word. Megan jerked toward him, but Cameron clutched the device in his hand, holding it by his shoulder as a silent sign he wasn't giving in.

Her deep red lips parted in protest before her shoulders sank and her hands fell to her lap. Megan's head drooped. With all her hair tucked back, he could see every emotion that slid over her face, even though he could only see her profile. Her eyes closed, she bit her lip and her chin trembled. She looked positively defeated.

That right there was why Cameron loathed Evan Richards. The man constantly deflated the life out of fun-loving, bubbly Megan. Moments ago, when she'd stood in Cameron's hallway, she'd been sassy, confident and vibrant...everything he loved. What he didn't love was how quickly one person could bring her down. Evan was nothing but a bully, always seeking his own selfish desires and not giving a damn who he hurt along the way.

"Don't you dare feel bad," he scolded, maybe harsher than he should have. "That's exactly what he wants, Meg. He plays that guilt card with you because he knows you'll give him anything he wants."

"I know," she mumbled. Smoothing her hands down her fitted skirt, she let out a sigh and turned to face him. "I'm trying, really. It's way past time he stood on his own two feet. It's just so hard..."

She shook her head and reached for the keys in the ignition. After sliding his hand over her slender arm, Cameron gripped her hand.

"That's what he's counting on." Cameron gave her a gentle squeeze as he softened his tone. She wasn't a perp; she was his friend. "He continually plays the poor sibling, expecting you to ride to his rescue. He's the one who made this mess of his life."

Cameron seriously doubted she knew just how much of a mess Evan was in. There was no way he could protect her from the end result. The helpless feeling in the pit of Cameron's stomach nearly made him sick.

Tears brimming in her eyes, she held his gaze. "You think I don't know how much Evan has screwed up? That he doesn't use me on a daily basis? You don't know what I go through, Cameron. You have the picture-perfect family. I have no parents and a brother who'd just as soon wipe out my bank account as spend five minutes talking with me on how to straighten his life out, how to help him. I'm praying maybe one of these times he comes to me, he'll be there for more. I'm praying he'll let me help him, that he'll be ready to turn his life around. So if I have to get stepped on along the way, it's worth it."

The last sentence came out on a choked sob. Well, hell. Now he was the one feeling guilty. He never wanted to make her cry, make her feel as if his life was better than hers.

After placing her phone back on the console, Cameron reached across and wrapped his arms around her the best he could, considering their positions.

"I'm sorry." Her silky hair tickled his cheek, and her familiar floral scent reminded him she was nearly everything to him and he'd die before he'd hurt her. "I don't mean to be hard on you. I just hate seeing what he does to you."

Megan's hands slid up his torso between his jacket and his shirt, coming to rest against his chest. "What I deserve and what I'll have are two different things."

Easing back, Cameron studied her face. "You deserve everything you've ever wanted."

A sad smile spread across her face as she reached a

hand up and cupped his freshly shaven jaw. "All I've ever wanted may not want me back."

What?

Before he could question her further, her hand fell away and she started the vehicle. Whatever secret longing she kept locked deep inside was obviously something she'd all but given up on. Cameron refused to let Megan give up on any dream or goal she had.

He vowed that once this major case was over, he'd find a way to make her happy, living the life she desired and deserved. It would be worth everything to him. For years he'd seen her always put her needs behind everyone else's. And while he may not be the man to settle into her life intimately, he would do everything in his power to make sure her dreams were fulfilled.

Chapter Two

"I'm so glad you could make it."

Bev St. John hugged Cameron after the christening service, then looped her arm through his as they walked back up the wide aisle of Santa Monica Church.

"You don't know how much this means to me to have all my boys here for my first grandbaby's milestone," Bev said, her wide smile spreading across her face.

Straight ahead, near the tall double doors, Nora and Eli stood with Megan. Megan held his infant niece, who was just over a year old. Cameron's heart filled. The glow on Megan's face as she placed a kiss on top of Amber's curly blond head solidified the fact he couldn't be the man for her. She would be an amazing, loving, selfless mother. Just not to his kids.

Cameron's dad, Mac, approached and looked over Megan's shoulder, smiling down at his granddaughter. Cameron didn't know where Megan would be if it weren't for his family. She'd taken to them even before her parents had died suddenly, but she'd really leaned on them during that difficult time. Even as strong as Megan was, she'd been so blindsided by the shock of losing both parents, and then taking over the care of her younger brother when she'd barely gotten out of high school herself. "I'm so glad Megan could make it." His mother's soft tone pulled him back. "I just love that girl."

Over the years his mother had made it no secret she wouldn't mind Megan being part of the family—in the legal, choosing-china-patterns type of way. Of course now that Eli and Drake were taken, his mom would just have to settle for Megan being a friend and the daughter she'd never had.

Cameron steered them toward the little grouping, and Megan glanced up, caught his eye and smiled. Yeah, there was that invisible pull once again that threatened to wrap around his neck and strangle him.

He wanted her. Wanted her so much sometimes he physically hurt. But she deserved more.

The memory of the darkest time in his life took over. His partner had taken a bullet meant for Cameron. On his last breath, his partner had made Cameron promise to make sure his wife knew he loved her.

That moment changed everything. Letting a woman into his life, letting her get close enough to be devastated like his partner's wife had been, was not something he'd ever take a chance with. If he entered into a deeper relationship with Megan and something happened to him, it would kill her. Besides, worrying about her while he was trying to do his job was a sure way for him to get hurt. He needed to concentrate, needed to keep Megan out of his mind.

If he could only figure out how the hell to do that.

"Megan, you look beautiful, as always." His mom leaned forward and kissed Megan's cheek. "Thanks for being here today."

"I wouldn't miss it."

"Are you and Megan coming to eat with us after?" Eli asked Cameron. "We're heading to that new Italian place just outside of town."

Cameron started to agree, but Megan chimed in. "I have to get home, but if you want to go, go ahead."

Oh, no. If she was going home to wait on her freeloading brother to show, Cameron would be right there with her. No way would Evan try to pull her into this latest mess. Hell no.

"I need to head out, too," Cameron stated. Work was always beckoning, so he knew everyone would just assume that's why he needed to go. "And she's my ride."

Cameron and Megan said their goodbyes and stepped out of the church. The bright sun hit them as they descended the concrete steps. Cameron pulled his glasses from his jacket pocket and slid them on to block the brightness. A headache from lack of sleep and plenty of worry had settled in, and the fiery glare was making it worse.

"Skipping out?"

Cameron turned to see his other brother, Drake. Right at his side was his fiancée, Marly, and Marly's daughter, Willow.

"Megan and I need to head out," he told Drake.

"You look pretty," Willow said, standing beside Megan and looking up at her as if she were looking at a movie star. "I like your hair."

The free-spirited little six-year-old had on her beloved cowgirl boots, as usual, and was sporting a new grin, sans two teeth.

Megan bent down and slid her hand through Willow's long ponytail. "I love yours, too. I used to wear my hair just like this when I was your age. You have good taste."

"I was going to call you," Marly told Megan. "Nora and I were hoping for a girls' night sometime soon. You interested?"

Megan smiled and nodded. "Sounds good. Just let me know when."

More goodbyes were said, and finally Megan and Cameron were settled back in her SUV and headed toward their neighborhood.

"That was a beautiful service," she commented after a bit. "Thanks for inviting me."

"You're family." Cameron tried to hold back the yawn but couldn't. Damn, he was getting too old to pull all-nighters. "You belong here, too."

"You know, one day you may actually replace me with a girlfriend or a wife. I doubt she'll understand if I'm still hanging around your family."

Cameron snorted, shifted in his seat and rested his

elbow on the console. "For one thing, you could never be replaced. For another, I think you know my stance on committed relationships and marriage."

"Your reasons may be valid, but they can't be your crutch for life."

"It's not a crutch," he muttered in defense.

Megan threw him a glance and a smile as she pulled onto their road. "You never know when the right woman will come along and claim you."

The only woman he'd ever allow to "claim" him was sitting right next to him, but he'd never do that to her. He'd seen firsthand what being a cop could do to even the strongest of marriages. Even though he and Megan had a bond that rivaled the toughest relationships, he wouldn't put that kind of strain on something, or someone, so important.

She was part of his life in the deepest way he could allow and he'd just have to be satisfied with that. The fact she would likely marry one day was something he couldn't even think about right now. If he thought of Megan with another man, Cameron would likely lose that wall of control he'd built up.

Megan put on her signal to turn into his drive.

"I'm going to your house," he told her.

Totally ignoring him, she pulled up to his garage. After throwing her SUV in Park, she turned to face him, her green eyes studying his face. "You need to go in and get more sleep."

She was preaching to the choir. Unfortunately, even if he went in, he wouldn't be able to just close down and relax. Besides, he wanted to make sure Evan didn't show up and try to pour on more guilt or ask for any favors.

"I'll be fine," she assured him, patting his leg as if he were some toddler. "I know what you're doing, but don't worry. I've handled Evan long enough."

Cameron slid his hand over hers and squeezed. "And that's the problem. You shouldn't have to deal with a grown man whose behavior is that of an out-of-control teen."

Megan tilted her head, and her hair spilled over her shoulder; the strands tickled his arm on the console. "I deal with you, don't I?"

He couldn't help but smile. "You only keep me around to set your mousetraps in the winter."

"True." With a smile, she turned her hand over in his and squeezed. "Seriously. Go sleep."

Stroking his thumb along the backs of her smooth fingers, Cameron stared into those eyes that were too often full of worry—eyes that had captivated him on more occasions than he could count.

"I'm a guy and a cop. I can't help but want to take care of you."

Drawing in a shaky breath, she offered a sweet smile, one he'd witnessed for years and never grew tired of seeing. Megan's genuine, contagious smile that came from within, that lit up a room...that's what kept him going.

"I love you for that," she told him. "But really, you need to take care of yourself, and I'm going to make sure you do. Now go."

Stubborn woman. She wouldn't pull out of this

driveway until his butt was out of her car. *Fine.* He was just as stubborn, but he knew how to play the game. He knew his Megan better than anyone else did. She would always put herself out to make others comfortable, to keep those around her happy. But Cameron wasn't about to let her fall down his priority list. She was, and always had been, at the top. Just like family.

"All right," he conceded. "You will call me if you need anything."

It wasn't a question, but she nodded anyway as she leaned over to kiss his cheek. "Go on, Chief. You can't protect the town if you're dead on your feet."

"Yes, Mommy."

Cameron tugged on the handle and stepped from the SUV. Turning to rest his arm on the open door, he peered back inside. "You know, tough love is a good thing."

"Yeah." Megan sighed, and her shoulders fell slightly. "It's just easy to say and harder to do."

Cameron hated how torn she was between loyalty and forgiveness. He, too, was torn between loyalties right now. Megan had been his everything for so long. Yet he couldn't protect her, couldn't even warn her of the evils hovering so close to her life.

Tapping the top of her car, he stepped back. "I'll call you later."

As he made his way up to his porch, Cameron knew he wouldn't be sleeping. Too much was on his mind, and it all involved work and Megan. She always seemed to be the center of his thoughts. Unfortunately, this scenario had nothing to do with his desires.

Yet Megan's odd declaration earlier alluding to something or someone she wanted still weighed heavily on his mind, too. They shared everything…at least all the personal stuff. What was she keeping from him?

Granted, he'd been holding back his own feelings for so long, but he didn't think she reciprocated those emotions. Or did she? That would put a whole new spin on things and add another layer of worry to his already stressful life. Damn it, why couldn't he just have those friend feelings or that brotherly bond? When had he taken that turn into wanting more?

Cameron waited until Megan headed down the narrow road toward her own house before he turned in the opposite direction and took off for a much-needed walk around their neighborhood. He needed to clear his head and figure out how best to approach this delicate situation with Evan.

Cameron also needed to figure out how to get the image of Megan in that classy yet sexy-as-hell red dress out of his mind. No other woman could shoot for polished and timeless and come off as a siren. Megan's beauty had always been special, but today she'd taken it to a whole new level. The more time passed, the deeper his feelings went. There was nothing he could do; he'd tried denying it, tried ignoring it. Unfortunately, Megan had embedded herself so deeply into his life that he had no clue how to function with all of these lies.

Yeah, a walk was definitely what he needed to get his head on straight because losing himself in his thoughts where Megan was concerned was only throwing fuel on the proverbial fire. Too often when they were close together in a car, on her sofa watching a movie, he'd fought not to kiss her, not to touch her. The struggle he battled with himself was a daily occurrence, but he'd sacrifice anything, even his desires and his sanity, to keep her happy and safe.

Lust, love or anything other than a simple friendship had no room in the well-secured bond they'd honed and perfected since childhood.

So focusing on this case from hell that had just taken a turn for the worse was the only thing he had time to dwell on. Because in the end, no matter his feelings for Megan, she would hate him for standing by and watching her brother make mistake after mistake, for waiting to take down him and his criminal friends. But Cameron didn't have a choice. His job had to come before his feelings for Megan.

Clothes were strewn around her room, hanging over the treadmill, draped across her bed, adorning the floor mirror in the corner. Pretty much every stationary object had taken a hit from the purging of her closet.

Megan tugged on the black tank-style dress that used to be her favorite. When she gave a pull to cover her rear end, it pulled the scoop neck down. When she tried to pull the material up over her breasts, her butt nearly popped out.

Damn that new Ben & Jerry's flavor. Ice cream was her weakness, and now she'd discovered something else to feed her addiction…and her thighs.

So here she was, going through her closet because she needed to de-clutter. Nobody needed this many clothes, and she'd gained a few pounds, so why keep all this stuff? If she ended up losing the extra weight, she deserved a shopping spree, anyway. And if she opted to take that new job in Memphis, she would want to start fresh. That meant getting rid of this too-tight, hoochie-mama-looking dress.

Besides, reorganizing her overflowing closet was a great stress reliever and a good way to keep her mind off Cameron.

With a laugh, she fingered through the pile of too-small clothes on her bed. Like Cameron was ever off her mind. She'd nearly slipped up and bared her soul to him earlier when he'd declared he wanted her to have all she'd ever desired. Could the man be so blind that he couldn't see she desired him? Did he pay no attention to the fact she rarely dated and when she did it was only one date because nobody could ever compare with Cam?

She knew why he didn't go out with women. He was married to his job. But he'd never questioned her on why her social life was nonexistent.

Or perhaps she was the blind one. Maybe she wasn't ready to face the fact that he truly didn't want anyone in his life, and even if he did, she would only be a friend to him.

Though he had given her a visual sampling when he'd first seen her before the christening. That was a good sign…right? Or maybe he'd just had indigestion from all the garbage he ate the night before. Who knew?

Groaning, she started to attempt to get out of the

body-hugging dress when she heard her back door open and close. Jerking around, she tried to listen to the footsteps.

Evan? Cameron? Either way she was clearly not dressed for company.

"You wearing pants?"

A slight sigh of relief swept through her as she laughed at Cameron echoing her earlier question to him. Her body was half hanging out, but extra pounds or not, men usually just saw skin and got excited. Could this work to her advantage? Maybe being a bit more out there, literally, would get Cameron to wake up.

"Actually, no," she called back, then stepped into the hall to tell him she'd be right out.

As soon as she left her room, she ran into Cameron's solid chest. Firm, strong hands immediately came up and gripped her shoulders. Her breasts, already spilling out of her dress, pressed against his hard pecs. Megan sucked in a breath, unable to think of anything but how nicely they molded together in all the perfectly delicious ways.

The way his eyes widened, his nostrils flared and his fingertips bit into her bare skin told her he wasn't so unaffected by her femininity.

Game on.

Chapter Three

Holy—

Cameron couldn't breathe, couldn't think, couldn't form a damn thought with Megan's curvy body pressed against his. This was his best friend, yet with the way her breasts were all but spilling out of her barely-there black dress, his thoughts weren't very friend-like at the moment.

Hadn't he just pep-talked himself into trying to keep his thoughts out of the gutter?

"Wh-what are you doing here?" she asked.

Why was her voice all breathy and sultry?

Cameron dropped his hands and took a step back, but that didn't help his hormones settle down. Now he was able to see just how hot she looked wearing that second-skin dress that hit her upper thigh at a very indecent level and scooped low enough to show off her breasts.

Jealousy ripped through him. "Where the hell are you going like that?"

She flinched. Maybe he'd sounded a tad gruff, but seriously? Every visual that came to mind involved a bedroom.

Megan lifted her chin defiantly as she crossed her arms, doing nothing to help her cause of breast spillage. "For your information, I'm cleaning my closet and trying things on. Now, why are you here and not home asleep?"

He was starting to question that himself. "I couldn't sleep."

Not that he'd tried, but she didn't need to know that. He glanced into her room and laughed. Megan always had everything in its place, but something tragic had transpired with her clothes. He wasn't dumb enough to make a comment because he was pretty sure that some rage had been unleashed in that room.

"Not a word," she growled, as if daring him to comment on the chaos. "Let me change real quick."

Before she turned away, the back door opened and closed. Cameron nearly groaned. Nobody else would just walk in other than him or Evan.

Megan let out a sigh. "Be nice," she whispered. "I'll go change."

Cameron turned away just as Evan rounded the hall corner. His disheveled hair and black eye were so predictable. He looked like a deadbeat who'd obviously been on the wrong end of one of his "friends'" fists.

Cameron wouldn't allow him to come in here and make Megan feel like crap.

"Am I interrupting something?" Evan asked, his narrowed eyes darting between Cameron and Megan.

Cameron wanted to tell the guy yes, but he didn't figure Evan would leave and the lie would only make Megan upset. No matter what, he was treading a fine line because if this weren't Megan's only living relative, Cameron wouldn't think twice about hauling his butt in if for nothing else than to shake him up a bit.

Megan stepped into her room and came out seconds later tying a robe around her waist. At least she was covered now. Cameron didn't like that judgmental glance that Evan had thrown at them. Even if Cameron and Megan had been doing something intimate, that wouldn't have been Evan's business...or anyone else's for that matter.

"What happened?" Megan asked, stepping toward her brother.

Evan waved a hand, his eyes still moving between Cameron and Megan. "Nothing for you to worry about."

Cameron knew those blow-off comments hurt Megan. The woman obviously cared for her brother, and Evan didn't even acknowledge the fact.

"I do worry," she told him with a softer tone.

Cameron maintained his place between the two siblings. No way was he budging. When it became clear that Evan wasn't going to offer any more feedback over his recent fight, Megan sighed.

"What do you need, Evan?" Megan asked as she took a step back, landing her next to Cameron.

Good. Cameron wanted her to feel safer with him there. The silent gesture clearly showed who she trusted, who she felt more comfortable with. The primal part of Cameron liked to think her easing closer to him showed whose side she was on, as well.

"I need to talk to you," Evan told her, then shifted his eyes to Cameron.

"Go ahead," Cameron replied, resting his hands on his hips and in absolutely no hurry to budge.

"Alone."

Megan moved down the hall, squaring her shoulders. "I'm not giving you money," she informed him as she got closer. "If you want to visit with me, that's fine."

Evan raked a hand through his hair, then threw another glance at Cameron and back to Megan. Cameron didn't move, didn't even consider giving them privacy because he wanted Megan to know he was here for support. He wouldn't chime in, wouldn't say a word unless he saw she couldn't be strong. But he had faith in her. He knew she was getting tired of her brother only coming around for money.

Evan leaned down, whispered something to Megan and gripped her arm. Cameron went on full alert.

"No, Evan," Megan said softly, shaking her head. "I don't have it to give. I'm sorry."

"You're not sorry," he spat as he released her with a forced shove. "I don't need that much."

Megan stumbled back a step, but caught herself as she crossed her arms and tipped her chin. "I have obligations, too, Evan. I can't always give you money because you get into trouble."

Evan's focus darted over Megan's shoulder, and Cameron merely narrowed his eyes, silently daring Evan to cross the line. The arm incident was more than enough to have Cameron ready to smash his face, but Megan wouldn't like Cameron interfering. Plus as an officer of the law, Cameron couldn't just go around punching all the people who pissed him off. Such a shame.

Cameron would like nothing more than to show Evan some tough love, but Megan was right. That was easier said than done. And as much as Cameron loathed the man, he *was* Megan's brother and she loved him.

"I'll come back when we can talk in private," Evan said, looking back to Megan.

"My answer won't change," she informed him. "But you're always welcome in my house."

Evan merely grunted and started to turn.

"I love you," Megan said, her voice shaky.

Evan froze, didn't look back, didn't comment, just paused before he disappeared around the corner. Moments later, the back door opened and closed again.

Megan turned, a fake smile pasted across her face, and started down the hall toward her room, skirting around him. "Well, let me change and then maybe we can do dinner. You want to go out? I'm not sure I have a lot here—"

Cameron followed her into the bedroom and watched as she jerked off her robe and tossed it onto the mound of clothes on her bed. As she glanced into the mirror and sighed, Cameron came up behind her, resting his hands on her shoulders and meeting her gaze in the reflection.

"You don't have to pretend with me."

Her bright green eyes held his. "I'm not pretending," she assured him. "I'm ignoring the fact that for years I've been an enabler to someone who really doesn't care about me, and I'm done. I'm also starving, so while I change, figure out what you want to eat."

Cameron knew there was so much more in her, but he wasn't pressing the matter...not when she was staring back at him with such vulnerability and was half-naked. They were back to that damn body-hugging dress again, and Cameron didn't know if he wanted to keep looking or if he wanted her to cover up.

Megan's entire body relaxed against his. Her bottom nestled against his groin, and Cameron tried to ignore the innocent gesture as he wrapped his arms around her shoulders and held her securely. She needed comfort, needed to lean on someone even though it was against everything she stood for. She'd never admit she needed to draw from his strength, but Cameron was freely giving it.

Unfortunately, his fingertips barely brushed across the tops of her breasts before he could complete his hold. A shiver racked her body and vibrated through his.

"I'm glad you're here," she whispered, her eyes still locked on his in the mirror.

Looking at her reflection was quite different from being face-to-face. He didn't know why, but in the mirror he saw so much, too much. Her vulnerability stared back at him at the same time that her killer body mocked him. He was her friend, damn it. He shouldn't be having these thoughts of how perfect she felt against him, how sexy she was.

"I wouldn't be anywhere else." Even though his libido was taking a hard hit, it was the truth.

With a deep breath, Megan straightened and turned, all but brushing those breasts against his chest. Okay, really. He was a guy already on the brink of snapping the stretched line of control, and there was only so much more of this he could take.

"Are you working tonight?" she asked, oblivious to his inner turmoil.

"No." He dropped his arms to his side and took a slight step back, away from that chest, the killer body that was slowly unraveling him. "Why don't I run to the store and grab something while you change?"

"A night in?" She beamed. "Only if I get to pick the movie."

Cameron groaned. "If I have to watch *The Godfather* again…"

With an evil laugh and a shrug, Megan stepped around him and started digging through clothes. "You choose the meal—I choose the movie. You know that's how we work."

Yeah, that's how they worked. They'd been working like this for years, before his deployment and since. But in all the years they'd had this routine of spontaneous date nights with each other, never once had the urge to peel her out of her clothes been this strong.

Of course now that he'd seen her, held her and visually enjoyed her in this dress, he could think of little else. So in a moot attempt at holding on to his sanity, and their friendship, Cameron conceded.

"You win," he told her. "I'll be back."

Even if he removed himself from the situation, Cameron knew he was screwed. Now that he'd seen her lush, curvy body, and felt it so intimately against his, he couldn't *not* see it. The image, the feel of her, was permanently ingrained into him.

Penance for his sins of lying to her.

Every single time they settled in for a movie, Megan fell asleep within the first hour without fail. Tonight was no exception.

She'd curled her feet beneath her, rested her head on his shoulder and before the mobsters could leave the gun and take the cannoli, Megan was out.

Cameron propped his feet up on her coffee table and slid farther down on the sofa. Carefully, he adjusted Megan so she lay down, her head on his lap. Resting his own head against the back cushion, Cameron shut his eyes and attempted to relax. Her delicate hand settled right over his thigh as she let out a soft sigh.

With his hand curled over her shoulder, feeling the steady rise and fall, Cameron realized he actually preferred resting just like this to his bed at home. At least here he had company. At home he had thoughts that kept him awake and staring at the ceiling fan. Work never fully left him—occupational hazard.

But here, with Megan, he could let work shuffle to

the back of his mind. He didn't want to burden her with his stress, so he purposely tried to be a friend first and a cop second whenever he was with her. Added to that, he reveled in the fact she was comfortable and sleeping soundly. He wanted to be her protector, her stable force. Somehow knowing he was all of that allowed him to let down his guard just a bit.

Crossing his ankles, Cameron rested an elbow on the arm of the couch. He'd muted the movie once Megan had fallen asleep, but the flicker of the screen lit up the room. As always, when they had movie night, all lights were off.

A shrill ring pierced the silence, and Cameron jerked awake. The TV had gone black, indicating he'd dozed off for a good bit, but he didn't really recall how long ago that had been. The ring sounded again. He grabbed his side, but Megan's phone on the table was the one lit up. Normally his phone was the one that rang at all hours.

She was still out with her head on his lap. He didn't recognize the number on the screen. Shocked the caller wasn't her brother, Cameron nudged Megan's shoulder.

"Meg."

She groaned and rolled to her back, blinking as she looked up at him. The sight of her utterly exhausted and rumpled from sleeping on his lap shouldn't have his body stirring. Damn that red dress from the christening and the skimpy number she'd had on earlier.

The third ring ripped through the silence, and Megan was on instant alert. She jerked up, grabbed the phone and answered.

Cameron shifted his legs to the floor, immediately getting some blood flow back. They'd obviously been asleep for a while, which was what they had both needed.

Megan came to her feet and spoke in hushed tones as she walked into the other room. He assumed it was a client. Megan often counseled long after regular office hours were over. She was so good at her job because of how caring she was, how much she sacrificed to make sure her clients' needs came first.

Cameron got to his feet, then twisted at the waist until his back popped in all the right places. He was getting too old to sleep on a couch, a car, his office. Unfortunately, he didn't see an end to his bad habits anytime soon.

He turned off the TV, sending the living room into utter darkness. Megan rounded the corner from the kitchen just as he started to reach over and click on the lamp, but his hand bumped the stand and sent the light to the hardwood floor. He cringed at the racket.

"Don't move." Megan turned on the kitchen light, sending an instant glow shining into the living room. "Let me grab my broom."

"You're barefoot," he told her. "Let me clean it up."

"You don't have shoes on, either." She disappeared down the hall and came back with broom and dustpan in hand. "Sit on the couch, and I'll get this."

Like hell. Ignoring her, he reached down to pick up the cockeyed lampshade and the remains of the lamp. The bulb and base had completely shattered.

"I'll bring you a new one later." He set the awkward

shade and lamp guts on the coffee table and reached to take the broom.

Stepping around him, she handed him the dustpan and started sweeping. *Stubborn woman.* No wonder they were best friends. Nobody else would put up with how hardheaded they both were.

He squatted down and held the pan while she scooped in the shards. "At least this wasn't a family heirloom," he joked.

Shoving her hair from her eyes, she threw him a glance. "Funny."

Cameron headed into the kitchen to toss the debris. As he was tying the bag, the vacuum kicked on in the living room, the occasional cracking noise indicating she was removing the rest of the slivers from the floor.

He tugged the liner from the trash can and tied it, wanting to get it out so she didn't cut herself later. As Cameron jerked the knot in place, a hunk of glass he hadn't seen poking from the small hole sliced through the edge of his hand.

Damn. That hurt.

He opened her back door, tossed the bag into the larger can on her patio and closed and locked the door. The vacuum shut off in the other room as Cameron headed to the sink. Running his hand beneath the cool water eased the burning sensation and washed away the mess, allowing him to see just how deep the cut was. Megan didn't need to know he'd hurt himself. She'd make a bigger deal of it than need be.

After rinsing his hand, he examined the area further. Instantly he started bleeding again. Apparently it was deeper than he thought.

"Hiding something?"

Cringing, Cameron ripped off a paper towel, pressed it against the side of his hand and turned toward his accuser. Megan rested one shoulder against the door frame, arms crossed over her chest, and merely lifted a brow.

"Just a scratch." That hurt like hell. Apparently he was old and wimpy. Great combo for the police chief.

Cameron's eyes locked on to her shapely legs as she crossed the room. *Damn it.*

Carefully, she took his hand and pulled the paper towel away. "Oh, Cam. This needs stitches."

She examined his hand, then brought her gaze up to meet his. In the middle of the night, with everything so quiet and intimate, Cameron knew for a fact he was starting to delve into a territory he had no business being in.

Her eyes held his, dropped to his mouth, then traveled back up. That gesture said more than any words could. But this was Megan, his best friend, the girl who'd been his senior prom date and the girl who'd sneaked out with him and his brothers that same night and got absolutely plastered near the lake.

She was pretty much family. So why was she looking at him beneath those heavy lids? Why was he enjoying this rush of new sensations, wondering if she had deeper feelings? He shouldn't want her to have stronger emotions for him. That added complication was the last thing either of them needed.

"Come with me."

Cameron blinked. "Excuse me?"

Megan smiled. "To the bathroom. You're too stubborn to go get stitches, so I'll fix you up with my first-aid kit."

When she turned and headed back down the hall, Cameron released a breath he hadn't been aware he'd bottled up. Had he been the only one thinking about what would happen if they kissed? The way she'd looked at him, his mouth, as though she wanted more, wasn't something he'd made up. But the desire flashing in her eyes was gone in a second.

What was going on in that head of hers? More to the point, what the hell was he going to do if her feelings did match his?

"Cam?"

Pushing off the edge of the counter, Cameron moved through the kitchen. They were both sleep deprived; that was all. He'd been without a woman for so long, was so wrapped up in work, and Megan had quite a bit on her plate, as well.

Once daylight came, once reality settled back in and the ambience was gone, this intense moment would be forgotten. Wouldn't it?

Chapter Four

Megan squeezed her eyes shut and willed her hands to stop shaking. That was a close call. She'd nearly ignored every single red flag waving around in her mind and kissed Cameron.

She'd been examining his hand one second and the next she'd found herself lost in those St. John signature blue eyes. After just coming off a phone call with one of her teen clients, Megan had wanted to lose herself in Cameron, even if only for a moment. Bad idea, bad timing.

Heavy footsteps sounded down the hall. Megan stepped aside to give Cameron room. Her guest bath was the smallest in her house, but it was where she kept her first-aid kit.

Without a word he came in and sat down on the

edge of the garden tub. If she thought the bathroom was tiny before, having a man of Cameron's size there only solidified the fact.

"I can take care of this at home," he informed her. "It's the middle of the night."

Ignoring him, Megan cleaned the area, concentrating on her task and not the enclosed space or the warmth radiating from Cameron's body…or the fact she stood directly between his spread legs and only had on a tank and a pair of old boxers.

You'd think she'd at least take a bit more pride in her appearance when he came over, but this was Cameron. He knew her better than anybody so if she donned something halfway dressy, he'd wonder what was wrong.

Megan feared she'd doomed herself into the friend category for life where Cameron was concerned. She'd had feelings for him for years, yet the man was utterly oblivious.

Once the area was clean and dry, Megan quickly placed butterfly bandages over the cut. The strips weren't nearly as effective as stitches, but she wasn't fighting with the stubborn man. Men were like children—you had to pick your battles.

Megan turned to throw away the used supplies and wrappers, only her body and her mind weren't in sync and she swayed slightly. Strong arms circled her waist, holding her steady in an instant.

"You okay?"

Nodding, Megan closed her eyes as his caring words

and warm breath washed over her. "Yeah. The room started spinning for a second. I'm just tired, I guess."

With a gentle power she'd come to appreciate, he eased her down onto his leg. Megan twisted to face him, wondering if this would turn awkward. She didn't want awkward anywhere near their perfectly built relationship. They'd been friends too long to allow anything negative or evil to slip in.

When Cameron's uninjured hand covered her bare thigh, Megan's first thought was how she was glad she'd shaved that day…or the day before, considering it was after midnight.

Her second thought was that she hoped he didn't feel her body trembling beneath his touch. Unfortunately, keeping her body controlled around Cameron was impossible.

"Was that call earlier from a client?" he asked, his thumb tracing an invisible pattern over her thigh.

Staring into those eyes, Megan could only nod.

"You're working yourself too hard, Meg." His bandaged hand slid up, pushing her hair off her shoulder and down her back. "I know you want to be there for your patients, be there for your brother, but when will you do something for yourself?"

Actually, being on his lap right now fell nicely into the "doing something for yourself" category.

"Are you the pot or the kettle?" she asked with a smile.

A corner of his mouth tipped up into a tired grin, causing the corners of his eyes to crease. "Whichever one you aren't."

Megan yawned. "Sorry. You want to crash in the guest room tonight?"

"I'll just walk home."

As Megan came to her feet, Cameron stood with her and kept a hand on her waist.

"Dizzy?" he asked.

Shaking her head, Megan started putting the first-aid kit back. "I'm fine. I've just not been sleeping lately and with the call and then your injury, I think my body was trying to crash before I was ready."

Without even looking at the man, she knew his eyes were on her. She could feel them, feel him.

"Is your client all right?"

Megan thought back to the call. No matter how many years she'd been counseling, certain topics never got easier to deal with, and there were those special cases that truly touched her heart. Megan wished more than anything she could wave a magic wand and heal all the hurt she dealt with on a daily basis.

"Honestly, no." Megan put the kit back under the vanity. She leaned back against the counter and crossed her arms over her chest. "She's unstable, scared and can't live a normal teenage life. It's not fair and I want to go get her and bring her here. She needs love and guidance and to be able to sleep without worrying about her family."

After taking one step, Cameron stood in front of her. His good hand came down and rested on the edge of the sink beside her hip.

"You can't make up for the past, Megan."

How easily this man could see through her. He

knew how she equated every teen to her brother when he'd been an out-of-control hellion after their parents' deaths. Still, the day Megan quit caring about her clients would be the day she quit her job.

"I can't," she agreed, trying not to think about how close he was, how his breath tickled her face or how his body was nearly covering hers. "But I can help one person. I can help steer them toward a better future."

Cameron wrapped his other arm around her shoulders and pulled her against his hard chest. Tilting her head to rest her cheek against him, Megan inhaled the familiar masculine scent. What she wouldn't give to be able to wrap her arms around him and have the embrace mean so much more than friendship. An embrace that led to something intimate, something that would take them to the next level.

"Why don't you concentrate on getting sleep for what's left of the night?"

Megan eased back and smiled. "You sure you don't want the spare room?"

Cameron shook his head and took a step back. "I need to be back at the station early. I'll just head home."

A sliver of disappointment slid through her, but Megan kept smiling. Seriously, if he stayed it wasn't like she'd make a move, even though she'd thought she was ready to admit her feelings. Why couldn't she be more forward about what she wanted? She admired women who targeted a man and went after him.

Megan walked him to the door, rubbing her tired, burning eyes. "If that hand still looks bad by afternoon I want you to think about getting stitches. I'm not a nurse, you know."

Cameron glanced down to the bandage and shrugged. "It's not my shooting hand. I'll be fine."

Rolling her eyes, Megan reached around him and opened the front door. The living room and foyer were still only illuminated by the light spilling in from the kitchen.

"I have a crazy schedule the next couple of days, but I swear I'll get that lamp replaced."

"Don't worry about it." Megan covered her mouth as another yawn slipped out. "I'll just take one from the spare room until I get to a store. No big deal."

The screen door creaked open as Cameron stepped onto her porch. A cool breeze drifted through as he turned and studied her once more. He opened his mouth as if to say something, but he ended up tightening his lips. Megan wanted to know what he was thinking after they'd shared those intense moments.

Finally he swallowed and nodded. "Lock up behind me."

Megan reached for the screen door to prevent it from slamming. "Always."

"You've got to be kidding me."

Cameron crossed his arms over his chest and stood back, admiring the gaudy gold dragon lamp he'd found on his lunch break at one of the antiques stores in town.

"What?" he asked, pretending to be offended. "It puts out more light than the one you had—plus it was only eight bucks."

Megan laughed. "You got screwed if you paid more than a dime for that hideous thing."

"So you'd rather pay more for something that does the exact same thing?"

Megan stepped closer, bending down to inspect the new piece. She wrinkled her nose, squinted her eyes and her mouth contorted into an expression that looked as if she'd just inhaled the sickening aroma of a sewer plant.

This was the exact reaction he'd expected...which was why he'd bought the ugly thing.

"You did this on purpose," she accused, turning her scrunched face to him. "You know how I am about gifts, and you know I'll keep it just because you got it for me."

Cameron shrugged. "Maybe. Do you still have that unicorn salt-and-pepper-shaker set?"

Her eyes narrowed as she crossed her arms and mirrored his stance. "You know I do. I just don't get it out of the cabinet."

For years he'd randomly bought her tacky things from time to time just for a laugh. He knew how she treasured every present because she hadn't had much growing up and gifts were few and far between. Megan had a loving heart, and she'd never give away something someone bought her.

And now this tacky dragon lamp, with the light shooting out of the open mouth directed toward the ceiling, adorned her neutral-toned living room. A dragon that projectile vomited light? This was a new level of tacky. Cameron had to really bite the inside of his cheek to keep from bursting out laughing.

"I thought you were too busy to see me today."

The list of things Cameron needed to do flooded his mind. Tonight he'd be staking out another parking lot, waiting for the familiar crew of drug runners to pass through. Cameron only hoped Evan wasn't with them this time. He truly hoped Megan's brother would get away from that crowd. This case would not have a positive ending, and Cameron didn't want to arrest Evan and help convict him of a felony. That crushing blow would kill Megan.

"I'm on my way back in," he told her. "But when I saw this, I just knew you had to have it. I couldn't wait to see your face."

"There will be retaliation," she promised with a gleam in her eyes.

"I can't wait," he retorted, laughing.

Rain started splattering the windows as the gray clouds moved over the sun, blocking out the natural light.

"Got this lamp in just in time," he said, not even trying to hold back his grin. "It's supposed to storm all night. It'll be good for you to sit in here and read."

"I'd hate for the power to go out and my lamp to have some malfunction due to the storm."

Cameron patted the top of the beastly thing. "This is an antique. I'd say she's been around through many storms. Don't worry."

"She? You're giving that thing a gender?"

Cameron may have initially been drawn to the lamp

because of the shock factor and the entertainment value of presenting it to Megan, but there was more. After he'd gotten over the amusement, he realized in some weird way, this dragon reminded him of Megan. Sturdy and fierce. Of course, if he mentioned any of that to her she'd probably launch the heavy atrocity right at his head.

"You can give her a name," he added, just wanting to get under her skin. The unladylike growl was perfect. "Think about it. No need to call her anything right now. You'll want to acquaint yourself."

"I'm thinking of a few names," Megan said through gritted teeth. "None of them are for her, though."

Cameron swatted her arm. "See? You're already thinking of the lamp as her. You'll have her named by the end of the day."

Another unladylike growl escaped Megan as her eyes narrowed to slits. "Don't you have a city to protect?"

More so now than ever, yet he found himself not wanting to leave. This was the first time in a while he actually smiled for good reason. Added to that, he felt they needed this ridiculous moment after way too many close calls. His control was about to snap.

Even if he had wanted to risk their friendship and delve into a more intimate relationship, he couldn't ignore the flashes of his old partner that ripped through him. The man had been married to his job and he'd had a beautiful young wife at home. Now she was a widow. Cameron tried to check in on her from time to time, and he would never forget her face when she'd learned her husband had been killed in the line of duty. Killed by a bullet meant for Cameron. The guilt used to eat at him, but now he realized he would've done the same thing. Jumping into the line of fire wasn't something you thought about, you just did it.

"Cam?"

Megan's hand on his arm and her soft tone pulled him from his thoughts. "Yeah. Sorry."

"You left me for a minute." Her arched brows drew in. "You can talk to me. I know you can't discuss open cases, but you can at least get out some frustration."

No, he couldn't because the second those words left her lips, he found himself studying her mouth. The very thought of kissing her should have made awkwardness rise to the surface, but he found himself curious how she would taste, how she would respond. There was only one way to get her out of his system.

"I'm fine," he assured her. Well, as fine as he could be considering he was now fantasizing about kissing his best friend and keeping the fact that her brother was in way over his head with drug runners a secret. "I need to get going."

Megan reached out, wrapping her arms around him. She held on tighter than usual and damn if that didn't send a shot of arousal straight through him. Cameron slid his arms around her waist, loving how she just knew when he needed a connection most.

"Be careful," she whispered just before she stepped back. "I know you're working on a big case, but promise me you're cautious."

Cameron swallowed, hating the worry that settled

in her bright eyes. This was the reason he wouldn't subject her or any other woman to his line of work.

"I promise," he told her. "Text me and tell me what you name her."

Megan's eyes darted to the dragon lamp and back to him. "Distracting me from worry won't work."

Cameron gave her shoulder a squeeze and headed to the door. "No need to worry. Call me if you need anything."

"You know I won't call you." She smiled and tipped that adorable defiant chin up a notch. "I'm perfectly capable of taking care of myself."

Yes, but she didn't know what she was up against if her loser brother opted to somehow use her in his latest dealings. Cameron had to be on full alert because the likelihood of Evan trying to get something from Megan or bringing the rest of the cronies into her life was viable. Cameron might be watching the entire city, but his focus was zeroed in on keeping Megan safe and oblivious to the activity hitting way too close to home.

Granted, this was a small town, but that didn't mean evils wouldn't try to reach their arms in and infiltrate anyone who proved to be an easy target. Cameron wouldn't allow his town to be overrun by corrupt, illegal activities as long as he was chief.

Cameron headed back to the station, where he would be meeting up with an FBI agent to discuss the case. Too often cops developed inflated egos and didn't want outside assistance. Cameron wasn't that stupid. When the FBI had come in, he had welcomed the extra help. He'd do anything to keep his town safe, to keep drugs from filtering into the schools and homes of innocent, unsuspecting kids.

He wasn't naive enough to believe he could stop all drug trafficking, but he was damn sure going to stop this group from bringing shipments into Stonerock. Every bust, every seller taken off the streets, could possibly be saving someone's life.

Cameron couldn't wait for this case to wrap up. They had a good amount of evidence so far, but they needed a bit more. An undercover FBI agent had been placed deep in the runners' inner circle months ago. Another reason Cameron was elated to have them all on board.

All they had to do was wait on his signal, and then the group would be taken down.

Glancing back at Megan's one-story cottage, complete with cheery colorful flowers and a yellow front door, Cameron only hoped he could save her from the pain of seeing her own brother in prison. Unfortunately, Cameron didn't think that was possible.

Chapter Five

The storm had ripped through the night, putting off the surveillance. Cameron and a few other officers and FBI agents had waited around the station, hoping the storm would pass. Unfortunately, with lightning bolting across the sky and claps of thunder raging at the same time, even the dealers weren't stupid enough to be outdoors.

At around three in the morning, Cameron headed home, ready to get a few hours of sleep before coming back. Their informant had told them another meet was scheduled to happen in three days. Cameron honestly thought of taking a day off to do absolutely nothing. He was running on fumes. All he wanted to do was fall face-first into his bed and sleep for a good solid eight hours. Was that too much to ask?

He and the other agents and officers were convinced

it would only take one or two more meets before they could bring the group down. The day wouldn't come soon enough.

His headlights cut through the darkness as he pulled into his drive. He needed a shower and a bed. He actually needed food, but that would have to wait. He was too exhausted to even pry open a package of toaster pastries at this point.

After letting himself in the back door, he removed his shoulder holster and gun. After carrying it through the darkened hall, he stepped into his bedroom and placed the gun on the dresser just inside the door. Turning around, he went into the bathroom directly across the hall from his room.

The shower was quick, hot and enough to loosen his sore muscles and have him one step closer to falling into oblivion as soon as he slid between his sheets.

Wrapping the towel around his waist and tucking the edge in to secure it in place, Cameron padded back across the hall. He kept his blackout shades pulled at all times, seeing as how he never knew when he'd get shut-eye and he wanted to keep the room nice and dark. Of course tonight, with the storm, the moon wasn't even out to offer a glow.

Cameron jerked off the towel and hung it on the closet doorknob. Shuffling toward the king-size bed, Cameron nearly wept at the thought of falling asleep. Now, if he could stay asleep that would be a miracle.

Jerking back the covers quickly revealed two things: there was a woman in his bed, and there would be no sleep tonight.

* * *

His hands glided over her bare skin, sending ripples of satisfaction coursing through her. Finally, after all these years, she would finally know what making love to her best friend was like.

A soft groan escaped her lips; her body arched in eager anticipation.

"Megan."

Even his voice aroused her. That low, throaty tone. She'd imagined him growling her name while looking into her eyes as his body leaned over hers.

"Meg."

The firm grip on her shoulder had her lifting her lids, blinking. Darkness surrounded her, but the shape before her was so familiar, so close. She reached up, slid her hands over his stubbled jaw and pulled him down. Her mouth covered his and for a second she wondered why he wasn't responding.

The thought was fleeting as Cameron's hesitant state snapped; his hold on her shoulders tightened. His mouth opened, his tongue plunging in to tangle with hers. Yes, this is what she needed, what she craved.

The weight of his body pressing hers back into the bed, the sheer strength of this man, consumed her in every single way and made all her fantasies seem so minor in comparison.

The euphoria of coming from a dream into reality—

Megan froze. Dream into reality? *Oh, no.* She had been dreaming earlier...now she wasn't.

As if sensing her detachment, Cameron stilled and lifted his head. She lay on the bed, the top half of his body covering hers, the tingling sensations still rippling through her as she focused back on the cold, harsh reality.

"Cam?"

"Yeah." His husky voice did nothing to rid her body's ache. "Um…sorry. That was…I don't…why did you kiss me?"

With her palms plastered to his bare chest—his bare, damp chest—Megan closed her eyes and battled with telling the truth or saving her pride.

"I was dreaming."

Pride won out. How could she tell her best friend she'd been dreaming of seducing him and fully succeeding? How could she tell him that for years she'd dreamed of taking control and making him see just how amazing they'd be together?

"That was one hell of a dream." He eased himself off her, and as her eyes fully adjusted to the darkened room, she realized he wore… *Oh, mercy.* He wore absolutely nothing.

Embarrassed, yet incredibly still aroused, Megan shoved her hair away from her face. "I didn't want to bother you at work and I thought I'd be gone by morning since I figured you'd be out all night." She realized she was rambling, but nerves had taken over and she'd lost all control. As she rambled, though, it gave him time to retrieve a towel from the closet knob and secure it around his waist. "I couldn't sleep at my house and had you been home I would've taken the couch, but since you were out…"

Cameron smiled as she trailed off, and she figured

she sounded as nervous as she felt. Silence settled between them, and he crossed his arms over his chest, as if wearing only a towel was the most comfortable thing in the world.

Was he not affected at all by that kiss? She knew for a fact he'd been somewhat aroused when he'd been on top of her, but now he merely looked at her with that lopsided grin she'd come to love.

"I don't mind a bit that you came here," he informed her. "But what was wrong with your house?"

Restless on so many levels, Megan came to her feet and started smoothing out the covers. "My back door had been tampered with and the lock was broken. I wasn't comfortable sleeping there. I didn't figure you'd mind."

"What the hell, Meg?" Reaching around her, he clicked on the bedside lamp. "Someone broke in and you were afraid to call my cell?"

"I wasn't afraid," she defended herself, testing every bit of her self-control as she kept her eyes on his and not on the stark white towel riding low on his hips or the sprinkling of dark hair across his bare torso. "I knew you were busy and…can you put some pants on? I can't talk like this."

A corner of his mouth kicked up into a grin. "You've seen me in swim trunks, Meg."

Yes, but in those instances he hadn't just been lying on top of her, kissing her back as if she were his next breath of air. Would her lips ever stop tingling from all that heat? His body's imprint was permanently ingrained onto hers.

Her eyes darted to the bed, re-creating an image of how close she'd been to attaining her greatest fantasy. When she glanced back up, Cameron's jaw was clenched, his eyes holding hers as if he knew exactly where her thoughts had traveled and he was having a hard time keeping his own from going there.

"It's not the same," she whispered.

With a nod, he turned, pulled a pair of shorts from his drawer and slid them on beneath the towel. With a flick of his wrist, the towel came off and he hung it back on the doorknob before he crossed the intimate room to stand within a breath of her.

"Now, tell me what the hell is going on. What happened at your house?"

Megan pulled in a deep breath, giving herself an extra minute to figure out how to control her emotions and get back on track to where their conversation needed to be.

"My back door had been kicked in or something. It was open and the lock was busted."

Cameron raked a hand over his still-damp hair and muttered a curse. "You'll call me next time anything happens. Me, not the department, not another officer. You'll call my cell."

A little surprised at his demanding tone, Megan propped her hands on her hips. "What would you have done? Left whatever you've been working undercover on for months?"

His narrowed eyes held hers as he eased forward just enough for his bare chest to brush against her. "Yes."

He'd put work second? That was a first. Work never

came after anything for Cameron. He took pride in keeping his town's reputation favorable and the crime rate low. To know he would've dropped everything for her caused a new warmth to spread through her, overlaying the previous heat from their intimate encounter moments ago.

"I didn't need to call you for a busted door," she said. "I knew you'd look at it sometime in the morning. I just wanted to sleep. Like I said, had I known you'd be home, I'd have taken the couch."

While his small cottage had two bedrooms, the second bedroom was full of workout equipment that aided in bulking up his already magnificent physic.

"I'll take the couch," he told her. "Go on back to sleep."

Oh, sure. As if she could crawl back into that bed after what had just happened. She'd had a hard enough time getting to sleep in the first place because she'd nearly suffocated herself by burying her face into his pillow and inhaling that familiar masculine scent. She really needed to get a grip before she made a complete fool of herself.

"I'll take the couch." She smiled up at him, hoping the friendly gesture would ease the tension. Granted, the tension was most likely all one-sided. "You've been up long enough and there's no way you'll fit."

"What kind of gentleman and friend would I be if I booted my best friend to the couch?"

Best friend. Had he thrown those two words at her to remind her of their status? Had she completely freaked him out when she'd attacked him, rubbed herself all over him and claimed his mouth? Part of her was mortified; the other part of her was a bit relieved she'd finally kissed him. She'd not only kissed him, she'd full-out devoured him. But now she knew how he tasted, how he felt. That knowledge was both a blessing and a curse.

"I either take the couch or I head home where it may not be safe."

True, she wasn't fighting fair because no way would he let her go if he thought for a second she wasn't well protected. He studied her for a moment, and Megan tried not to look away or fidget beneath that hypnotic gaze. Would she ever stop tingling? Would she ever forget how perfectly his body felt pressed against hers? She hoped not. Those were memories she'd want to re-live over and over for as long as possible.

"You're stubborn."

Megan shrugged. "One of my many talents," she told him, patting his bare shoulder because she was having a hard time resisting all that glorious skin mere inches away. "Sleep tight."

Inching around him, inhaling that fresh-from-the-shower scent, Megan made her way out of his room and headed to the couch. She may as well just head on home because there was no way she could sleep now, not after that kiss. But she would stay. If Cameron knew she was home, he wouldn't rest, either, and he desperately needed to before he worked himself to death.

Megan pulled a blanket from the back of the couch, fluffed the throw pillow and lay on her side, facing the hallway. The darkened space offered nothing of comfort or peace. The silence was equally as empty.

Was Cameron already lying in bed? Had he already slid between the sheets she'd just come from? Had that kiss even made an impact on him, or was he completely repulsed at the fact his best friend had tried to consume him?

More than likely the man's head had barely hit the pillow before he was out. At least one of them would get some sleep tonight.

Chapter Six

How the hell could a man rest after finding a woman in his bed, being kissed in such an arousing way by said woman and now smelling her fruity scent on his sheets?

Cameron laced his fingers over his abdomen and stared up at the ceiling fan. Whoever Megan had been dreaming about was one lucky man. The way she'd all but plastered her curvy body against his had him instantly responding. Hence the problem with sleeping. How the hell did he react to this? For a few brief moments, he'd found something with Megan he'd never experienced with any other woman. Ever.

What was the protocol for discovering your best friend kissed like every man's fantasy? He knew he'd wanted her on a primal level, but to actually have evidence of the fact only added to his confusion.

This was Megan, the woman who knew all his secrets, all his annoying quirks. They'd been through everything together from riding their first rollercoaster to her brother's ups and downs.

She was like family, only he was feeling close to her in a way that had nothing to do with family. He'd secretly hoped if he ever got his hands or lips on her, he'd get her out of his system because he'd feel nothing. Unfortunately, that was completely the opposite of what had just happened. He felt too much, too fast.

Cameron's body still hadn't settled back down, and it wouldn't anytime soon. Who the hell had Megan been dreaming about? She wasn't dating anyone, unless she was keeping it a secret.

Damn it. Jealousy was an ugly, unwelcome trait.

Swiping a hand down his face, Cameron cursed himself. Here he was, dead on his feet, unable to sleep for fantasizing about his best friend dreaming about a mysterious man. How messed up had his life become in the past hour?

Licking his lips, he still tasted her. He couldn't want more. Wanting anything more from Megan was out of the question. Their friendship was solid—why mess that up just because she kissed like every dream he'd ever had?

Movement in the house made him focus on the darkness instead of his wayward thoughts. Bare feet slid over the hardwood. The refrigerator door opened, closed, followed by the sound of a cabinet being shut softly. She was trying to be so quiet, but he wasn't sleeping and he was trained to hear even the slightest disturbances.

This new tension that had settled between them wasn't going anywhere. She may have tried to act calm after what they'd shared, but he knew her well enough to know she was anything but. Her nerves and emotions were just as jumbled, just as buzzing, as his were.

With a sigh, he sat up and swung his legs over the side of the bed. Might as well face this head-on. He didn't want uneasiness to become an uninvited third party in their relationship. Maybe she really was just dreaming, but the way his body responded, the way she'd been jittery afterward, told him there was more.

He padded his way down the hall, his eyes adjusting to the darkness in his familiar surroundings. The living room was empty, so he turned toward the kitchen, where he saw her. Leaning against the counter, looking out onto the backyard, Megan held a glass in her hand. Cameron studied her in a new light. He couldn't deny her beauty, with her perfectly shaped curves and hair that tumbled down her back. Those green eyes could pierce you in an instant, and now he knew that mouth could render a man speechless.

Still clutching the glass and staring, Megan hadn't moved one bit since he'd stood here. Something, or someone, consumed her mind.

"Who is he?"

Megan jumped, turned and the glass she'd been clutching dropped to the floor with a crackling shatter.

"Damn it." He started to move forward but stopped. He reached around the doorjamb and flicked on the light, blinking against the bright glare. "Don't move. Neither of us have shoes on."

First the lamp at her house and now this. They hadn't even delved into relationship territory, and already things were breaking all around them. A metaphor for things to come?

He ran back to his room and shoved his feet into a pair of tennis shoes at the foot of the bed. When he got back to the kitchen, Megan was bending over, picking up pieces of glass.

"I told you not to move," he growled, not knowing which situation he was angrier at.

"I didn't take a step. I'm just picking up the large pieces."

He jerked open the small built-in utility closet and grabbed the broom and dustpan. After sweeping up the majority of the glass, Megan set the shards she'd held into the dustpan, too.

After dumping the mess into the trash, he went back and scooped her up into his arms without a word.

With a squeak of surprise, Megan landed against his chest and he had no idea how to react to the fact his body warmed and responded with her against him once again.

"This is overkill—don't you think?" she asked, sliding one arm around his neck.

"I need you out of the way so I can get the rest and you're not wearing shoes. So no, I don't think it's overkill."

He deposited her on the couch in the living room and made his way back to clean up the water and make sure all the fragments were swept up. Several minutes later, he headed back into the living room to find Megan gone.

Heading down the hall, he heard water running from the bathroom. She'd left the door open, allowing the light to spill into the hallway. When he peeked into the room, Megan was at the sink, holding one hand under the water. Blood seeped to the surface of her palm as soon as water could wash it away.

"Why didn't you tell me you'd cut yourself?" he asked.

"Like you told me the other day?" Throwing him a glance over her shoulder, Megan shrugged. "You were cleaning up the mess. Seriously, it's very minor. I could use a bandage, though."

Stepping forward, Cameron reached around, shut the water off and held on to her wrist to examine her hand. Her hair tickled the side of his face, and the pulse beneath his fingertips sped up. Gritting his teeth to shove aside any emotions outside the friend zone, Cameron inspected the injury.

"It is small," he agreed, still inspecting the area.

She glanced up, catching his eyes in the mirror. "It just needs to be cleaned up and a bandage. I wasn't lying."

When he continued to stare at her, she merely quirked a brow. Damn woman would make a nun curse like a sailor.

"Sit," he said, pointing to the toilet lid. "It's my turn to take care of you."

Grabbing the first-aid kit from beneath the sink, he

shuffled the supplies around and found what he needed to fix her up.

He took a seat on the edge of the tub and balanced the supplies on his thigh. With careful movements, he uncurled her fingers and examined the cut again. It was bleeding pretty good, but it wasn't deep at all.

"I'm thinking you and I need only plastic, child-safe things in our homes," she joked.

"At the very least, we should stop handling glass in the middle of the night."

Cameron appreciated her attempt to lighten the mood, but he'd come out of his room for a reason and he needed to get this off his chest.

"Why couldn't you sleep?" he asked, keeping his eyes locked on his task as he swiped her palm with gauze.

"Insomnia has become a close friend of mine lately."

That was something he definitely understood. Still, she'd been sleeping just fine earlier in his bed.

"I'll make sure your door is fixed so you can sleep in your bed." Confident the bleeding had slowed enough not to come through the bandage, Cameron held a fresh gauze pad over the cut and applied pressure. "I'm sorry I startled you earlier."

Her hand tensed beneath his touch. "What were you asking me when you came into the kitchen, anyway?"

Keeping his thumb over the pad, he lifted his gaze to hers. Those bright green eyes outlined by dark lashes held him captivated and speechless for a second. "Nothing. Forget it."

"You asked who he was," she went on. "What *he* are you referring to?"

Knowing she wouldn't back down, Cameron opted to face this head-on as he'd originally intended. He was chief of police, for crying out loud, yet the thought of discussing another man with Megan had him trembling and nearly breaking out into a sweat…not to mention ready to punch someone in the face.

"I wanted to know who you were dreaming about."

Megan lowered her lids, took a deep breath and let it out. "I'm not sure you're ready for that answer."

Not ready for the answer? What was she about to tell him? Was she fantasizing about someone he didn't care for? Cameron got along with nearly everybody on the right side of the law.

"It's none of my business," he repeated, not sure he was ready for the answer, either. "The way you kissed me…"

Megan stared at him as his words died in the crackling air between them. "I was dreaming of you."

Nerves and fear settled deep in her stomach as if weighted by an anchor. She kept her gaze on his, refusing to back down or show weakness. He wanted the truth—he got it. Now they would both have to deal with the consequences because she'd just opened a door and shoved him right on through into the black abyss. Neither of them had a clue what waited for them.

Cameron's warm hand continued to hold hers, protecting her injury. He clenched the muscle in his jaw as if he was holding back his response. Not knowing what was going on in his head was only adding to her worry.

"Say something." She tried for a smile but swallowed instead, blinking as her eyes began to burn with the threat of tears. *Oh, no.* She wouldn't break down. Not here, not now. "It was a kiss, Cam. No big deal."

Okay, so she'd tried to be strong and not back down, but right now, in the wake of his silence, she figured backpedaling was the only approach.

"Don't lie to me," he commanded. "I was on the receiving end of that kiss, and it was definitely a big deal."

Megan pulled her hand away and got to her feet, causing him to scoot back and try to catch all the supplies from his lap before they scattered to the floor.

"I was still asleep, Cameron. I was in your bed, surrounded by your scent. I can't help what I was dreaming."

Lifting the pad from her hand, she studied her palm. The cut only stung a little, not enough to keep her focus off the fact she was in this minuscule bathroom with Cameron and she'd just told him she'd been fantasizing about him. There wasn't enough air or space because he came up right behind her, practically caging her in between his hard, broad body and the vanity.

"So you're saying if I kissed you now that you're fully awake, you wouldn't respond like earlier?"

His bold, challenging question had her jerking her gaze up to meet his in the mirror. Slowly turning to face him, brushing against every plane of his torso in the process, Megan clutched her injured hand against her chest. Though the cut was insignificant in the grand scheme of things, holding on to it gave her a prop she needed to calm her shaky hands.

"It's late…or early," she told him. "Let's forget any of this happened and try to salvage what's left of the night. We both need sleep."

He braced his hands on the sink, officially trapping her in between his arms. "You're not a coward."

"No, I'm not. But this little exercise is ridiculous."

Lowering his lids, he stared at her mouth. "Then this won't be a problem."

His mouth slid over hers, and Megan pulled up every ounce of self-control to keep from moaning. Earlier she'd been half dreaming when she'd kissed him, but now she was fully awake and able to truly enjoy how amazing her best friend was in the kissing department.

Even though he was demanding and controlling, Cameron somehow managed to also be gentle with his touch. One strong hand splayed across her back, urging her closer. Her injured hand remained trapped between their bodies, and she fisted the other at her side because she didn't want to show emotion, not now. As much as she yearned to wrap herself around him and give in to anything he was willing to offer, she wasn't ready.

Cameron nipped at her lips, easing his way out of the kiss. But he didn't stop. No, the man merely angled his head the other way and dived back in for more.

The way he had her partially bent back over the vanity, Megan had to bring up her good hand to clutch his bare shoulder. She couldn't recall the last time she'd been so thoroughly kissed. No matter the time, she'd certainly never been kissed as passionately, as intensely, as now. Even those kisses that led straight to the bedroom had never gotten her this hot, this turned on.

Cameron fisted her T-shirt in his hand, pulling it tighter against her back as he lifted his head slightly. His forehead rested against hers.

"You're awake now," he muttered. "Feeling anything?"

Because she needed to think, and she knew *he* needed to think, Megan patted his shoulder and smiled. "You're a good kisser, Cam. No denying that. But I'm not dreaming anymore."

Cameron stepped back, hands on his narrowed hips where his shorts were riding low. "Tell me that didn't make your body respond."

She knew for a fact his body had responded, but she wouldn't be so tacky as to drop her gaze to the front of his shorts. They both knew she was fully aware.

Cameron had never even hinted he wanted to kiss her before. And even though she knew she should take this chance to tell him how she felt, she found herself lying to his face to save hers.

"Like I said, you're a great kisser," she told him. "But I've had better."

With that bold-faced lie, she marched from the bathroom and straight to the sofa, where she lay down facing the back cushions and covered up with the throw.

Megan wasn't quite sure if she'd put this experiment to rest or if she'd awakened the beast inside Cameron.

She had a feeling she'd find out soon enough. Thrills of anticipation coursed through her at the prospect.

Chapter Seven

Cameron needed this break. Between work and keeping track of Evan at various late-night meetings and that semierotic evening spent with Megan, he was about to lose it.

Drinking a beer on Eli's new patio with his brothers while their wives sat in the house discussing babies or shoes or some other frightening topic was exactly what he needed to relax.

Of course the incident with Megan had happened only two days ago and he still hadn't been able to get a grasp on how much that kiss, both kisses, had affected him.

"We've lost him again," Eli mocked, pulling Cameron from his daze.

"He's still working in his head." Drake took a pull of

his beer, then let the bottle dangle between his knees. "You're off the clock right now. Enjoy it."

Cameron rested his forearms on the edge of the deck railing and glanced out into the wooded backyard. Eli had built an addition on his home and then added the deck. He and his wife of nearly a year, and their baby, lived in their own little corner on the edge of town.

Drake, with his new bride and adorable stepdaughter, was embracing family life, as well. Drake had even mentioned how he and Marly wanted to try for a baby of their own.

Cameron couldn't be happier for his brothers, but they could keep their minivans, grocery lists and scheduled bedtimes. That wasn't a lifestyle he saw himself settling into anytime soon...if ever.

"I'm not working in my head," he defended himself. "I'm just enjoying listening to you two go on about recipes and paint swatches like a bunch of old ladies at a hair salon."

"Someone's grouchy," Eli muttered.

"Maybe he doesn't have a recipe worth sharing and he's embarrassed," Drake added with a low chuckle.

Cameron turned, flipping his brothers the one-finger salute. He missed getting together with them. They used to try to have a cookout or something once a week, especially since Eli's deployments were over and he was officially a civilian now, but Cameron's schedule was anything but regular. He hated putting work ahead of his family, but sometimes he couldn't help the matter. The criminals didn't seem to keep nine-to-five hours.

"Oh, hell," Drake whispered as he sat straight up in his deck chair. "You've finally got woman issues."

Eli's head whipped around, his gaze narrowing on Cameron. "Seriously? Because if you have woman issues, that means you have a woman, which is a damn miracle."

Finishing off his beer, knowing full well he needed something stronger to get into this discussion, Cameron tossed his empty bottle into the bin.

"I don't have a woman," he ground out, dropping onto the settee. "I have a headache over one."

Why did he have to go and issue Megan that challenge? Why did he have to push her into proving she was lying? Because all he'd gotten out of the deal was a hell of a great kiss, sleepless nights full of fantasies fueled by his best friend and a whole lot of anger with himself for crossing the line.

His own issues aside, how could he actually move to another level with Megan knowing her brother was well on his way to prison? Hell, Cameron was having a hard time keeping that bottled up now, and they were just friends. How could he keep secrets if he allowed intimacy to slip into the picture?

"Who is she?" Eli asked. "Oh, is it the new lady in town that lives out behind the grocery store? I hear she's single and if those tight-fitting clothes and spike heels aren't an invitation—"

"An invitation to what?" Nora asked from the patio door with her arms crossed over her chest, a quirked brow and a knowing grin on her face.

Eli cleared his throat. "Hey, babe," he said, crossing the wide area to wrap an arm around her waist. "I was just thinking about you."

She swatted him in the stomach. "If you think I'll ever dress like I work a pole every night, you're insane."

Eli groaned. "Please, don't mention a pole."

Cameron and Drake exchanged a conspiratorial look before they busted out laughing. "Still scarred from the image of Maddie Mays?"

Squeezing his eyes shut, Eli shook his head. "I'm trying to forget, but she was in again yesterday. Why does she always bring up her workout regime with me?"

"Because you're her doctor," Cameron smirked, enjoying the idea of his brother in such an awkward position. "Aren't you sworn to secrecy? I don't think you should share such things with us."

Eli blinked, narrowing his gaze. "If I have to suffer at the image, then so do you two."

"Mad" Maddie Mays had seemed to be a hundred years old when they were kids. At this point she may have been the same age as Noah and survived by hiding out on the ark. She'd never been a fan of the St. John boys and found their shenanigans less than amusing. More often than not, she'd chased them out of her yard wielding a rolling pin, baseball bat or sometimes both to really get her point across.

Now with Eli taking over their father's clinic, Maddie had no choice but to associate with at least one of the St. John boys, unless she wanted to find a doctor in a neighboring town. Apparently she'd warmed up to Eli. Perhaps sharing her unorthodox exercise routine was just her way of getting back at him for being a menace as a kid.

"If you guys are done discussing that poor woman, I wanted to know if you all had mentioned date night to Cameron." Nora took the bottle from Eli's hands and took a drink.

"What date night?" Cameron eyed his brothers. "You two aren't my type."

Nora smiled. "Actually we were wondering if you'd like to play the cool uncle while we went out. I was hesitant to ask you, but Eli and Drake assured me you wouldn't mind if you weren't busy."

Stunned, Cameron considered the idea, then shrugged. "Sure, I can do it." He'd just schedule the diaper changing and mac-and-cheese dinner around watching for drug smugglers. "How hard can watching a baby and a six-year-old be?"

His brothers exchanged a look and nearly turned red trying to hold back a comment or laughter. *Oh, they think I'm not capable? Challenge accepted.*

"Seriously?" Cameron went on. "You're already thinking I'm going to blow this? I run a town, for pity's sake. Surely I can handle two kids."

Nora stepped forward, patted his arm and offered a smile that was a bit on the patronizing side. Did nobody have faith in him?

"Just tell us when you're free," she told him.

Running his crazy schedule through his mind, Cameron knew there wouldn't be a great night, but he could surely spare a few hours. "I could do it Sunday evening."

"I work until four, but we could go after that," Drake chimed in.

"Great." Nora beamed. She leaned down, kissed Cameron on the cheek and patted his shoulder. "I'll go tell Marly."

She raced back into the house and Cameron leaned his head back against the cushion on the settee. Both brothers stared down at him.

"What?"

"You're not getting off the hook about this woman that has you tied in knots just because you're babysitting," Eli insisted. "We'll get the truth out of you one way or another."

Cameron didn't even know what there was to tell. Megan had kissed him, he'd kissed her and since then they hadn't spoken. What a mess, and most of it was his fault. If he hadn't insisted on challenging her, if he'd let her lie her way out of the first kiss, they would've moved on and ignored that pivotal turn they'd taken.

No way would he reveal Megan's name to his brothers. She was like a sister to them, and he wasn't sure they'd be on board with how Cameron had treated her.

But damn it, she'd tied him up in knots the second she'd slid her body against his.

"Come on—you can't sit there brooding and not fill us in." Drake leaned an elbow against the railing. "It has to be someone you know since you work every waking second. You don't have time to meet women unless it's someone you're arresting. Please, tell me you don't have some prisoner-guard romance going because if you do we're staging an intervention."

"Do you ever shut up?" Cameron asked, without heat. "Can't a guy keep some things to himself?"

"No," Eli and Drake replied in unison.

Raking a hand down his face, Cameron came to his feet. He couldn't stay any longer. If he did, they'd figure out who had him in knots and he couldn't afford to let that out right now, not when he was so confused. And he had no clue what was going through Megan's head, either.

"Now he's leaving." Eli laughed. "This must be bad if you're running from your own brothers."

"It's a small town," Drake added with a smile that stated he'd get to the bottom of it. "Secrets don't stay hidden long. The truth will come out eventually."

Cameron glared at his brothers before heading into the house to say goodbye to his sisters-in-law and his nieces.

The truth coming out was precisely what he couldn't have happen. But he knew he wasn't telling anybody about the incident and he doubted Megan would tell anyone, so that left the secret bottled up good and tight.

The question now was: When would it explode?

Megan hadn't even made it home from work when her cell rang. She'd just pulled onto her road when she answered without looking.

"Hello."

"I'm sorry to bother you."

Instantly Megan recognized the voice of one of her clients…a girl who'd just been in earlier that afternoon and the same one who'd called in the middle of the night days ago. Farrah wasn't the most stable person, and Megan made a point to really work with her. Megan cared for all her clients' well-being, but Farrah was extremely unstable and truly had no one else to turn to.

"Don't apologize," Megan insisted as she neared her driveway. "I'm here for you anytime."

"Earlier you told me that moving forward was the only way to start over."

Megan eased her car into the detached garage. "That's right."

Farrah sniffed. "I'm going to look for a job tomorrow. It's time I move out and try to make my life my own."

Megan had been waiting for Farrah to see that she needed to stand on her own two feet, to get away from the controlling man who held so much power over her. Megan had tried to stress how control can often quickly turn to abuse.

"I just wanted to thank you for today, and maybe… Could I put you down as a reference?"

Megan smiled as she killed the engine. "That would be fine. I'm really proud of you, Farrah."

Farrah thanked her, then ended the call. By the time Megan gathered her things and headed across the stone walkway to her back door, her phone was ringing again. She glanced at the screen and saw Evan's number. She hated how her first instinct was to groan.

How was it she could counsel total strangers, yet her own flesh and blood refused to take her advice or even consider for a moment that she wasn't trying to control him?

With a sigh, she answered as she shoved her key in her new doorknob. "Hi, Evan."

"Can I stay with you for a few nights?"

Stunned, Megan froze with her hand on the knob. She wasn't shocked at his abrupt question without so much as a greeting, but at the request. It was unusual for him not to ask for money first.

"Are you all right?"

"Yeah, yeah. I just…I need a place to crash. You going to help me or not?"

Closing her eyes, Megan leaned her head against the glass on the door. Even though his tone was put out and angry, he was at least coming to her for support.

"I'll always help you, Evan. But are you asking because you're ready to make changes in your life or because you're hiding?"

"Forget it," he grunted. "You're always judging me."

"No, Evan. I'm not judging—I'm worried."

Silence filled the line. Megan straightened and strained to hear.

"Evan?"

"If I wanted to change, could you help me?"

Now his voice came out in a near whisper, reminding her of the young boy he'd once been. At one time he'd looked up to her. When did all of that change?

"I'd do anything for you," she assured him. "Do you need help? I can come get you right now."

Again silence filled the line. She waited, not wanting to push further. This was the first time he actually sounded as if he may want to let her in. Megan prayed he would take the olive branch she'd been holding out for so long.

Commotion from the other end of the line, muffled voices and Evan's swearing told her the conversation was dead.

"I'll, uh, I'll call you later," he whispered as if he didn't want to be heard.

Gripping her phone, Megan pushed her way into the house. She didn't know why she'd let herself get her hopes up for those few seconds. She didn't know why she was constantly beating herself up over a man who might just continue to use her for the rest of their lives. But he was her brother and she would never give up. She may be frustrated and oftentimes deflated, but she wasn't a quitter and she would make damn sure he wasn't, either.

He'd called; that was a major step.

After hanging her purse on the peg by the back door, Megan slid her keys and phone inside. Her stomach growled, reminding her that she'd skipped lunch again in order to squeeze in one more client. Her supervisor kept telling her she needed to take breaks, but how could Megan justify them when someone's life could very well be in her hands? What if it was the patient who was contemplating suicide or leaving a spouse and they needed to talk right then? Megan couldn't turn them away.

Her eyes landed on the letter she'd tacked to the side

of her refrigerator. The letter outlining every detail for the new position she'd been offered in Memphis. The job was almost too good to be true, but it meant leaving Cameron, leaving the chance for something she'd wanted her whole life.

The directors had certainly pulled out all the stops to get her to take the position. The opportunity to help launch a free clinic in an area of town where people had been forgotten, left to their own devices. Megan wasn't married, didn't have kids and had been recommended for this job by her boss. How could she say no?

Two very valid reasons kept her from jumping at this chance of a lifetime: Evan and Cameron. Both men were fixtures in her life, and both men needed her whether either of them admitted it or not.

She hadn't spoken to Cameron in a few days, and emptiness had long since settled into that pit in her stomach, joining the fear and worry there. This was precisely why she hadn't made a move before, why she'd kept her feelings to herself. If a few kisses had already wedged an awkward wall between them, what would've happened had she told him she wanted to try a real relationship with him?

Megan glanced at the letter again and sighed. Maybe she should go. Maybe she needed to get away from the man who was a constant in her life but would never fill the slot she needed him to. And perhaps her new start would be the perfect opportunity for Evan to make a clean break, as well.

Chapter Eight

"I need you." Cameron surveyed the chaos around him and cringed. "How soon can you be at my house?"

Shrill cries pierced his eardrums for at least the fifteenth time in as many minutes. Every single parent in the world officially had his respect and deserved some type of recognized award for their patience.

"Where are you?" Megan asked. "What's all that noise?"

Cameron raked a hand over his hair and realized he needed to get a cut. He'd add that to the many things he'd slacked on lately. Right now, though, he was groveling to his best friend to come save him even though he'd been a jerk and hadn't spoken to her since.

His house was a complete war zone thanks to a spunky six-year-old and an infant.

Willow was dancing her stuffed horse in front of Amber's reddened, angry, tear-soaked face in an attempt to calm the baby, but Cameron figured that was only making it worse. Not to mention the fact that Willow had a slight goose egg on her head after tripping over the baby and falling into the corner of the coffee table.

Why had he insisted on watching the kids at his house? A house that was as far from baby proof as possible. He was a bachelor. Unfortunately, his bachelor pad had now tragically converted into a failing day-care center.

"Please," he begged. He never begged. "I'm home, and you can't get here fast enough. I'm…babysitting."

Okay, so he muttered that last word because he knew Megan well enough to know she'd burst out laughing and he wasn't in the mood.

"I'm sorry. Did you say *babysitting*?"

Cameron bent over and pulled Amber into his arms. "Front door's unlocked," he said right before disconnecting the call and sliding his cell back into his pocket. He had no time for mockery; this was crisis mode. Code red.

Megan would most likely dash down here within minutes, if nothing else to see firsthand how out of his comfort zone he was. The humiliation he was about to suffer would be long lasting, but at this point he didn't care. He needed reinforcements in the worst possible way.

This was not how he'd intended to apologize to Megan or how he'd planned on contacting her for the first time since he'd all but consumed her in his bathroom. Cameron hadn't mapped out a plan, exactly, but he knew he needed to be the one to take the next step. But the step he wanted to take and the step he needed to take were on opposite ends of the spectrum.

Cameron patted Amber on her back and tried to console her. How could someone so tiny be so filled with rage? Fatherhood was not his area of expertise. He wished there was some how-to manual he could read. Did Eli have this much trouble with his little girl? Cameron had never seen this side of his infant niece.

"Maybe you should sing her a song," Willow said, smiling up at him with a grin that lacked the front two teeth. "Do you know any songs?"

AC/DC's "Back in Black" sprang to mind, but he didn't figure an infant would find that particular tune as appealing as a nearly forty-year-old man did.

"I bet you know some," he countered. "What songs have you learned in school so far?"

Brows drawn, Willow looked lost in thought. Apparently, something brilliant came to her because she jumped up and down, her lopsided ponytails bouncing off her shoulders.

"'Wheels on the Bus'! That's my favorite."

After taking a seat on the sofa, Cameron adjusted Amber on his lap so the infant could see Willow and hopefully hear the song.

What else could he do? He'd fed her. Then she'd played on the floor with her toys, and now she was angrier than any woman he'd ever encountered on either side of the law.

Willow started singing, extremely off-key and loud, but hey, the extra noise caught Amber's attention and for a blessed moment she stopped screaming.

Then she started again, burying her face against his chest. Unfazed, Willow continued to sing.

The front door flew open, and Megan stepped in, instantly surveying the room. A smirk threatened to take over, but Cameron narrowed his gaze across the room, silently daring her to laugh.

He'd never been so happy to see another person in his entire life.

Willow stopped singing the second the door closed. "Hey, Megan. I didn't know you were coming over."

Megan smiled and crossed the room. "I didn't, either, but here I am."

Cameron tried to focus on the reason he'd called her here, but his eyes drank in the sight of Megan wearing a pair of body-hugging jeans and a plain white T-shirt with her signature off-duty cowgirl boots. With her hair pulled back in a ponytail, she looked about twenty years old.

Megan reached for Amber and held the infant against her body. Without giving Cameron another glance, she turned and started walking around the room, patting Amber's back and singing softly.

Well, what did he expect? He'd called her to help with the situation he obviously had lost control over, not to take up where they'd left off the other night.

Still, the fact she didn't say a word to him made him wonder if he'd hurt her more than he realized. He was botching up their relationship in every way, and he didn't blame her for being upset or angry.

Almost instantly the crying ceased. "Seriously? You hold her and she stops?"

Megan laughed, easing back to look Amber in the face. "I don't think it was me at all," she corrected him. "I think her stomach was upset. I just felt rumbling on my hand."

Cameron glanced to Megan's hand resting on Amber's bottom. Realization hit him hard. "Oh, no."

Willow giggled. "She feels better now."

Megan lifted Amber around to face Cameron. "She doesn't smell better," Megan said, scrunching up her nose.

Oh, please, please, please. There were few things that truly left him crippled, but the top of that list was changing a diaper…a dirty, smelly diaper.

Slowly rising to his feet, Cameron locked eyes with Megan. "I'll give you a hundred bucks to change that diaper."

Megan quirked a brow, her eyes glazed over with something much more devious than humor. "Keep your hundred bucks. I'll decide payment later."

Oh, mercy. Was she flirting with him? No, she was upset…wasn't she? Chalk this up to reason number 947 as to why he didn't do relationships. He'd never understand women. Ever.

"Where's the diapers and wipes?" she asked.

"Oh, I know," Willow raised her hand as if she were in school. "Follow me."

Megan trailed after Drake's stepdaughter and went down the hall to his bedroom. His bedroom.

"Don't change that diaper on my bed," he yelled. Laughter answered him, and he knew he was in for it. This was all part of his punishment.

The reeking smell in his bedroom was the least of his worries, because in just over an hour his brothers would be back to retrieve their kids—leaving him and Megan alone once again.

She should've left when everyone else did, but she'd put her pride and her emotions aside because she and Cameron needed to talk. He also needed help picking up his living room. Between the fort with couch cushions and blankets and the towels Willow had used as capes, making sure Cameron and Megan were superheroes, too, the place was anything but organized. The furniture had been pushed aside to allow room for "flying," and Megan hadn't even walked into the kitchen yet. She'd started making marshmallow treats with Willow just before she left and the mess was epic. She had to get in there before Cameron, with all his straight, orderly ways, had a heart attack.

Another thing she and Cameron saw eye to eye on. They both had a knack for cleanliness and keeping everything in its place…except for these emotions. They were all over, and nothing was orderly about them.

Best to start in the kitchen. Not only could she get that back in order, she could think of how best to approach being back in his house and all alone together…

Especially after that giant gauntlet she'd thrown down when he'd offered her a hundred bucks.

What had she been thinking? The flirty comment had literally slid out of her mouth. Clearly she needed a filter.

She'd been so amused by him babysitting, at the chaos his normally perfectly polished house was in. Then she'd seen him holding Amber and something very female, very biological-clock-ticking, snapped in her. She'd always known Cameron was a strong man who could handle anything. Yet the sight of those big tanned hands cradling an infant, of Cameron trying to console her with fear and vulnerability in his eyes, had sent her attraction to a whole new level. As if she needed yet another reason to be drawn to every facet of her best friend.

Surveying the cereal on the floor, Megan tiptoed carefully through to the other side of the kitchen to get the broom from the utility closet. In the midst of sweeping, a tingle slid up her spine and she knew she wasn't alone.

"Sorry." She went back to her chore, keeping her back to him. "Willow wanted to do everything on her own, so I let her. She's too cute to deny. I'll get this cleaned up and be gone."

When a warm, firm hand gripped her arm, Megan froze. Her heart kicked up, and she hated how she'd become this weak woman around her best friend. A part of her regretted sneaking into his bed. She'd cursed herself over and over for dreaming of him. The timing of the all-too-real dream at the same time he'd tried to wake her had thrown her control completely out the window.

But she couldn't wish away those kisses. No matter how she wanted things to be different between them right now, she would cherish those moments when his mouth had been on hers, his body flush against her own.

"Stop avoiding me." His low tone washed over her, and Megan closed her eyes, comforted in that familiar richness of his voice. "We haven't talked in days, and when the kids were here you barely said a word to me."

So she'd been using two innocent children as a buffer. What was a girl to do when she was so far out of her comfort zone she couldn't even see the zone anymore?

"You called me to help, so I helped." She started sweeping the dry cereal again, her swift movements causing Cameron's hand to fall away. "Let me get this cleaned up before you step on it and make it worse."

"Damn it, would you turn around and look at me? Stop being a coward."

That commanding tone had her gripping the broom, straightening her shoulders and pivoting, cereal crunching beneath her boots.

"Coward?" she repeated, ready to use her broom to knock some sense into him. "You could've contacted me, too, you know. How dare you call me a coward after that stunt you pulled? Did you think I'd wither at your feet or declare my undying love? What did you want me to say or do when you all but challenged me?"

She hated how anger was her instant reaction, but damn it, the man was dead-on. She had been a coward. She'd purposely not contacted him. Still, in her defense, he could've texted her or something.

"I'm not trying to start a fight." That calm, controlled cop tone remained in place, grating on her nerves even more because now she was fired up and he wasn't proving to be a worthy opponent. "I just wanted to talk."

"Fine," she spat. "You talk while I clean."

Angrier at herself for letting her emotions take control, Megan went back to focusing on the floor. With jerky movements, she had a rather large pile in no time. When she glanced out the corner of her eye and saw Cameron with his arms crossed over his chest, she had to grit her teeth to keep from saying something even more childish. The last thing she wanted was to be the reason this relationship plummeted, and if she didn't rein in her irritability about the fact he'd called her out, that's exactly what would happen.

Once she'd scooped up the mess and dumped everything into the trash, she put the broom and dustpan back in the closet. The counters weren't as bad, but the big brute was blocking them.

Propping her hands on her hips, Megan stared across the room. "You're going to have to move."

He moved—leaning back against the counter, crossing one ankle over the other. "You can't seriously be mad at me. Let's put the kissing aside, which I know for a fact you enjoyed. An hour ago you flirted with me and now you're ready to fight. What has gotten into you?"

The way he studied her, as if she were a stranger,

made her want that proverbial hole to open and swallow her. To be honest, she didn't know what had gotten into her, either. One minute she was ready to tell him her true feelings; the next minute she was angry at him for not reading her mind and at herself for being afraid to risk dignity.

Yeah, she was all woman when it came to moods and indecisiveness.

"We've already established the kisses were good," she agreed. "I didn't want your hundred bucks, and now I have leverage over you when I actually need something."

"I think you know I'd do anything for you," he told her. "You don't need to hold anything over me."

With a shrug, Megan went to the sink to wet the rag. "Fine, then get out of my way so I can clean and get home. I've had a long day, and I'm pretty tired."

She wrung out the water and turned, colliding with a hard, wide chest. Megan tipped her head slightly to look into Cameron's blue eyes. Those signature St. John baby blues could mesmerize any woman... She was no exception.

"Thank you for coming." He slid his hand up her arm, pushing a wayward strand of hair behind her ear and resting his hand on her shoulder. "I'm sorry for how I treated you the other night. Sorry I made you uncomfortable. But I'm not sorry I kissed you."

Megan heard the words, even processed what he was saying; she just couldn't believe Cameron was confessing this to her.

"Cam—"

The way his eyes locked on to hers cut off whatever she was about to say. The always-controlled cop she'd known most of her life looked as if he was barely hanging on. The level of hunger staring back at her was new. Had she misread him? Had he responded to that kiss in a way that mirrored her own need? Physically he'd responded, but what about emotionally?

"I won't lie and say I haven't thought of you as more than a friend before," he started. "I can't deny you're stunning, and you know more about me than anyone outside of my family."

Why did this sound like a stepping-stone to a gentle letdown?

"You don't have to defend your feelings," she told him, offering a smile. "I'm not asking for anything. I feel the same way."

Those strong hands came up to frame her face. "I liked kissing you, loved it, if I'm being honest."

Between that firm hold he had on her and his raw words, Megan wanted to let that hope blossom, but she wasn't ready to start celebrating just yet. The worry lines between Cameron's brows, the thin lips and the way he gritted his teeth between sentences were all red flags that he was in a battle with himself. Nothing spoke volumes like that raw passion staring back at her.

"Then why do you look so angry?" she asked.

His hands dropped to her shoulders, his fingertips curling into her skin. "Because this is such a bad idea on so many levels, Meg."

Heart beating fast, nerves swirling around in her

stomach, Megan forced all the courage she could muster to rise and take center stage.

"Why is that?" she countered with a defiant tip of her chin. "You're afraid of what it would do to our relationship? You think this is just some random emotion and it will pass?"

"Yes to both of those." His clutch on her shoulders lessened as he leaned in so close, his warm breath tickled her face. "And because if I start kissing you again, I won't stop."

Every nerve ending in her entire body instantly went on alert at his declaration. How could he drop a bomb like that and not expect her to react? Did he think he was helping matters? Did he truly believe with this knowledge she now possessed that she would give up?

"What if I don't want you to stop?"

By his swift intake of breath, she knew she'd shocked him with her bold question.

"You don't mean that," Cameron muttered.

Megan flattened her palms against his chest, slid them up to his shoulders and on up to frame his face. Touching him intimately like this was just the first step of many she hoped they'd take together. She wanted him to see she wasn't blowing this off anymore, wasn't pretending whatever was happening between them wasn't real.

"I mean every word. If you want something, why not take it?"

The way he continued to stare at her, as if listening to both the devil and the angel on his shoulders, made her take action into her own hands.

Rising to her toes, she pulled his head down and captured his lips with her own. She knew she'd made a good judgment call when Cameron instantly melted against her.

Chapter Nine

Every single valid reason for keeping his distance from Megan flew out the window with her lips on his. He'd always admired her take-charge attitude, but she'd never fully executed that power with him before.

He didn't know if he should be terrified or turned on.

Wrapping his arms around her, pulling her flush against his body, just seemed to happen without him even thinking. One second he was talking himself out of kissing her ever again. Then he'd touched her, and the next thing he knew she was on him...which wasn't a bad thing.

Cameron held one arm against her lower back, forcing her hips against his, and slid one hand up to the nape of her neck to hold her right where he wanted her.

Soft moans escaped Megan, and he couldn't stop the dam of need from bursting.

Bending her back, Cameron eased his fingertips beneath the hem of her shirt. Smooth, silky skin slid beneath his touch. The ache he had burning inside completely blindsided him. He'd known he'd wanted her, but the all-consuming passion that completely took hold of him was new.

Megan's hands traveled down to the edge of his shirt and the second her petite hands roamed up his abdomen, Cameron nearly lost it. It wasn't as if he hadn't been touched by a woman before, but never by the one woman he'd craved for years. Her touch was so much more hypnotizing than he'd ever imagined…and he'd imagined plenty.

Megan tore her mouth from his, tipping her head back and arching against him. "Cam," she panted.

Hearing his name on her lips in such an intimate way was the equivalent of throwing cold water on him. This was Megan. Evan's sister. A guy he was within days of arresting.

Cameron jerked back, his hands falling from beneath her shirt. Megan got tangled in his until he lifted the hem and took another step back.

Her moist, swollen lips seemed to mock him, showcasing what he'd just had and what he was turning down. He clenched his fists at his side, trying to grasp on to some form of control. Lately, where Megan was concerned, he was losing every bit of it.

"This can't happen."

Why did it sound as if his vocal chords were rubbing

against sandpaper? He couldn't put up a strong front if he didn't have control over his own voice.

Her eyes searched his, and Cameron hated the confusion laced with arousal staring back at him. Of course she was confused. He'd all but taken over the second she'd touched him and nearly devoured her; then he told her no and backed away as if she had some contagious disease.

Megan pushed off the counter. "What is the problem?"

Swallowing the truth, Cameron gave her another reason that was just as valid. "Sex would take us into a whole new territory. Who's to say that once we give in to this lust, that we won't resent each other or regret what happened?"

She crossed her arms over her breasts and shrugged. "Judging from that kiss, I can't imagine either of us would have regrets. So maybe we would actually enjoy ourselves and find that we may want to keep moving and building on our relationship."

That right there was the biggest worry of all. No way would he go through with this knowing he would have to tear her and her brother apart. Megan would hate Cameron when that time came, and if he slept with her now, she would hate him even more. He couldn't handle it. He only hoped their friendship would carry them over this hurdle once Evan went to jail and Megan understood that Cameron had no choice but to do his job.

Besides, if they went beyond the lust, beyond the sex, Cameron refused to let Megan lead a life married to a cop.

Married? Yes, he loved Megan more than any other woman, but marriage was not in his future.

"There's a reason I don't have relationships, Megan. You know that."

After staring at him for another minute, she laughed and threw her arms out. "So, what, you're just giving up before anything can get started? You're denying yourself, denying me what we both want because you already know the outcome?"

Pretty much.

"We can't come back to this after we have sex," he retorted.

"Come back to what?" she asked, taking a step closer, fire blazing in her eyes. "Friendship? We already crossed that threshold when your mouth was on mine and your hand was up my shirt."

Her angry, frustrated tone matched the turmoil raging inside him. What could he counter with when she was absolutely right? The second they'd crossed that line, an invisible wall had been erected, preventing them from turning back.

Why had he allowed this to happen? Why hadn't he let it go after she'd kissed him when she'd been dreaming? Even though she'd been dreaming of him, he could've moved on to save their friendship. But Megan's kiss had turned something inside him; something had clicked into place...something he couldn't identify because he was too scared to even try.

Megan threw her arms in the air and let out a low groan. "Forget it. Clearly you don't even know what you want. Or, if you do, you're afraid to face it. I don't have time for games."

"Games?" Cameron all but yelled, and he never yelled at anyone, let alone his best friend. "You think I'm playing a game here?"

When she started to walk by him, he reached out and snagged her arm until their shoulders were touching, her face tipping up toward his. The fury in her eyes wasn't something he'd seen too often and never before directed at him. Her chest rose and fell as her heavy breathing filled the silence. He didn't release his grip on her arm, apparently because he wanted to torture himself further by feeling that silky skin beneath his fingertips once more.

"Let me go," she whispered, her chin quivering.

Even with her eyes starting to fill, the anger penetrated through the hurt. As he watched her struggle with holding her emotions together, Cameron's heart jumped as he reluctantly slid his hand down her arm, stopping at her wrist and finally releasing her.

"I'm not trying to hurt you." That pitiful statement sounded flat and cold even to his own ears. "You're the last person I want to make cry."

A watery laugh escaped her. "You think I'm crying over you? These tears are over my own foolishness."

One lone tear slid down her cheek. Just as she reached up to swat it away, he caught her hand in his and used the pad of his thumb to swipe at the moisture.

He turned toward her and tugged her until she fell against him. Wrapping his arms around her, ignoring her protest, Cameron waited until she stopped struggling before he spoke.

"I don't want this between us, Meg. I can't lose you."

Her head dropped to his chest as she sniffed, her palms flattened against his shoulders. "This is just a really bad time, and my emotions are getting the best of me. Don't worry."

Cameron stroked her back, trying to ease all the tension, knowing he'd never fully get her relaxed and calm. But that wouldn't stop him from trying.

"You don't have to defend yourself," he muttered against her ear. "We've both had pressure on us lately. Finding you in my bed the other night and then kissing you, it was all unexpected and it takes a lot to catch me off guard."

Megan eased back, lifted her eyes to his and blinked. Wet lashes framed her green eyes as a wide smile spread across her face. "The fact that I manage to keep you on your toes after all these years makes me happier than it should."

The way she worded that, *after all these years*, sounded so personal. More personal than friendship. Married couples said such things to each other.

"I'm not blaming those kisses on pressure or the chaos in my life," she told him. "I realized soon after your lips touched mine that I wasn't dreaming anymore. I could've stopped, but it just felt so good and you were responding."

Hell yeah, he'd responded. He hadn't been with a woman for so long, but even he couldn't make that his excuse. Cameron had to at least be honest with himself. The second her lips had touched his, her arms encircled his neck, he'd been pulled under. All control had slid from him to her in the span of a second, and he hadn't minded one bit.

Then reality had come crashing back and he'd known what a mistake he'd made. Unfortunately, he'd gotten her in his system and now he was paying the price.

Damn it.

"I need to get going." She pulled completely away, eased around him and headed toward the living room. "The kitchen is done. Can you handle the living room?"

Why did his eyes have to zero in on the sway of her hips? Why was his body still humming from the way she'd been leaning against him?

Years ago he'd wondered, but he'd never made a move because either she or he had been dating someone. Then they got to a point where they were just perfectly happy being friends and not expecting anything more. He'd been deployed and hoped when he'd returned the feelings would've lessened. They hadn't. And then he'd become a cop, lost a partner and hardened his heart toward anything permanent.

So here they were, still best friends who each knew just how well the other one kissed. Cameron was also extremely aware of exactly how Megan liked to be touched and how hard and demanding she wanted those kisses. Her sighs, her moans, the way she arched her body against his were all images he'd live with forever.

He had to endure his own personal hell because he couldn't have her, wouldn't put her through coming in second to his job. And he damn well wouldn't expect her to want more once she learned he'd spent months bringing down a drug ring that now involved her brother.

Megan grabbed her keys off the small table just inside the entryway. "I'll be out of town Thursday and Friday," she told him without turning to look at him as she pulled open the door. "I should be home late Friday night."

"Where are you going?"

With her hand on the knob, she tossed her hair over her shoulder and stared back at him. "Just something for work."

Cameron curled his fingers around the edge of the wood door. "Is it a conference?"

"You might say that."

She was lying. Whatever she was doing, she didn't want to tell him.

"I don't expect you to share every aspect of your life," he told her. "But don't lie to my face."

Megan reached up, patted his cheek. "Kind of like you lying about not wanting more with me? That goes both ways, Cam."

Before he could respond, the cell in his pocket vibrated. *Damn it.* Now was not the time to deal with work unless it was to bring this ring down once and for all.

He pulled the phone out, saw his brother's number and didn't know if he was disappointed or relieved that work wasn't calling him in.

"Hang on," he told Megan. "It's just Eli. I'm not done with you."

Her eyes flared, and he realized how that sounded considering all that had transpired between them within the past week.

"What?" he growled into the phone.

"Mom fell." Eli didn't bother with any pleasantries. "I'm pretty sure her ankle is broken."

"Oh, hell." Cameron ran a hand down his face and sighed, meeting the concerned look in Megan's eyes. "Want me to meet you at the hospital?"

"I've already got her here," Eli answered. "You don't have to come, but I wanted to let you know what was up. Dad is home, and he's watching Amber for me. Nora came with me to sit with mom. Drake got called into work when one of his guys reported in sick."

"I'll be right there."

Cameron shoved the phone back in his pocket and yanked his keys from the peg by the door.

"Mom fell," he said, answering Megan's worried look. "Eli thinks her ankle is broken. I'm heading to the ER now. Dad is babysitting for Eli."

Megan stepped out onto the porch, holding the screen door open for him. "I'll go by your parents' house and sit with Mac and Amber. I'm sure he's worried. Keep me posted."

Before she walked away, Cameron reached out, wrapped his hand around the nape of her neck and looked her straight in the eyes. "I meant what I said. We're not done talking."

Megan's eyes locked on to his, her shoulders

straightened and that defiant chin lifted. "I'm pretty sure we're done discussing just how much you're denying both of us something that could be amazing. Until you're ready to face the fact you enjoyed kissing me, rubbing your hands on me, and admit you're just running scared, don't bring it up again."

She pulled away and bounded down the porch steps. "Just text with an update on your mom. No need to call."

And with that she headed toward her house, leaving Cameron to stare at those mocking hips.

Yes, he'd liked kissing her, thoroughly appreciated the feel of her curves beneath his hands. He was a man and she was a sensual woman whom he'd wanted for years. So what if he was running scared? Better to stop the disaster before it completely ruined their friendship.

As Cameron headed to his truck, he had a sinking feeling their friendship had already rounded a curve and was speeding out of control, and there wasn't a damn thing he could do about it.

Chapter Ten

"This fuss isn't necessary." Bev tried to maneuver her new crutches as Eli and Cameron flanked her sides, assisting her into the house. "I'll be fine. There's no need for everyone to hover."

"You will be fine," Eli agreed. "But for now we're going to hover. Just be glad Drake had to go in or you'd have all of us."

Megan held the door open with one hand and propped Amber on her hip with the other. "You know it's useless to argue with these guys, Bev," Megan said, catching the woman's grin. "Just let them think what they want to boost their egos."

Cameron's gaze swung to hers, and Megan merely lifted a brow. If he wanted to apply those words to the turmoil they had going on, so be it. Wasn't her fault if he had a guilty conscience.

Megan closed the door and pulled Amber around to settle against her chest as the baby continued chewing on her cloth rattle.

"I've already brought your pillows and pajamas down to the guest room," Mac stated, moving forward to take the place of his sons. "We'll be sleeping down here until you're healed and can do the stairs."

"And I'll be stopping by in the mornings," Nora stated, coming in through the door, holding Bev's purse. "I can do your grocery shopping after work so Mac doesn't have to worry about anything."

"One of my patients has volunteered to babysit Amber until you're feeling better," Eli added.

"Oh, for pity's sake." Bev stopped in the foyer and sighed, shooting glares at all those around her. "I can get through these next six weeks without rearranging everyone's lives."

Mac placed a hand over her shoulder. "Complain all you want, but when I had bypass surgery, you all steamrolled me and took care of me. Now it's our turn to cater to you."

A lump formed in Megan's throat at the sincere, loving way Mac looked to Bev. They'd always been such a dynamic couple, always strong even when dealing with hellion teen boys and all their shenanigans.

Megan knew that Mac's bypass surgery last year had rocked them all because the pillar of the family wasn't as indestructible as they'd all thought him to be.

Megan's eyes traveled to Cameron. Her breath caught in her throat when she found herself under the scrutiny of his bright blue eyes. Amber started fussing, pulling Megan's focus back to the infant in her arms.

"It's okay, sweetheart." Megan patted her back. "You're just getting sleepy, aren't you?"

Nora smiled, set the purse down on the accent table and reached out. "I can take her. She's not used to being awake this late."

"I'll run Eli home," Cameron chimed in. "Go on ahead and take her."

Nora said her goodbyes in a frantic attempt to get her unhappy child out the door. Once she was gone, Mac assisted Bev down the hall and into the spare room.

"I'll get her meds from the car," Eli volunteered. "She won't need any more tonight, but I'll put them in the kitchen where Dad can see them."

Eli headed out the front door, leaving Cameron and Megan alone. Why did they always somehow gravitate toward these situations? Before last week she wouldn't think twice about being alone with Cameron, but with all this tension crackling between them, she truly didn't know what step to take next. And she'd made it clear that the ball was in his court.

"I'm heading out," she told him. "Let your mom know I'm here if she needs anything. I'm free all weekend once I get back."

Cameron nodded. "Thanks for your help."

She waited for him to say something else, but he continued to stare in silence. Eli came back inside, carrying a small white pharmacy bag. He glanced between Megan and Cameron.

"Everything okay?" he asked, his brows drawn together.

"Fine," Megan and Cameron replied in unison, still eyeing each other.

"O-kay," Eli whispered as he moved on through to the kitchen.

Shoving her hair away from her face, Megan gritted her teeth as she reached into her pocket and pulled out her keys. Without another word, she headed out the front door and into the cool evening. She'd just hit the bottom step when she heard the screen door slam.

"Is this how it's going to be?" Cameron yelled. "This awkward, sometimes-polite chitchat like we're virtual strangers?"

Megan took in a deep breath before turning to face the man on the porch illuminated by the soft glow of outdoor lights. With his hands on his narrow hips, black T-shirt stretched tightly over toned shoulders and that perfectly cropped hair, Cameron gave off the impression of someone in control and pulled together.

Megan knew better. She'd experienced just how much he relinquished that power when she'd touched him, kissed him, pressed her body to his. And that interesting tidbit of information was something worth hanging on to.

The chill in the air slid through her. A shiver racked her body as she wrapped her arms around her midsection.

"If you feel awkward around me, then it sounds like you have some issues to work out," she threw back. She wasn't going to make this easy on him, not when he was being so infuriating. "I've always heard intimacy helps people relax."

Maybe she shouldn't poke the bear, but they'd already gone past the point of no return. She may as well toss it all out there.

Cameron took a step forward, his eyes still locked on hers. "Why are you acting like this?"

Megan shrugged. "Maybe that kiss was a wake-up for both of us, and I'm willing to face it instead of run from it."

Cameron bounded down the steps, coming to stand right in front of her. So close, she could feel his warm breath, but he didn't touch her.

"You keep coming to me," she added, looking up into those eyes filled with torment. "You keep provoking me, too, but then you back off. You can't have it both ways, Cam."

He gripped her arms in an almost bruising manner as he leaned over her, giving her no choice but to lean back to keep her gaze locked on to his.

Without a word, his mouth crushed hers. The instant demand had her clutching his shoulders and cursing herself for giving in to his impulses so easily. But damn it, she was human. She'd wanted this man for as long as she could remember, and she was going to take what she could get…for now. She wasn't settling for seconds; she was biding her time until Cameron realized this was right. Everything about them coming together was perfectly, wonderfully right.

Reluctant, Megan tore her mouth away. "If you're

only kissing me because you're angry with yourself or you're trying to prove a point, then stop."

His forehead rested against her temple, those lips barely touching her jawline. "I don't know, Meg. You make me crazy. I can't do relationships, and I won't do a fling—not with you. But part of me can't seem to stop now that we've started."

Not quite the victory she'd hoped for, but one she would definitely take. She had him torn, had him thinking. Still, she wanted, *deserved*, more.

"I won't be someone you figure things out with along the way," she told him, sliding her hands away from his taut shoulders. "If you want more, you say so."

She stepped back, waited until he looked at her before she continued. "Be damn sure if you come to me that you want what I've offered because there's no going back."

Megan waited, giving him an opportunity to respond. When silence greeted her and the muscle in Cameron's jaw moved, Megan swallowed, turned on her heel and headed to her car.

Maybe her going out of town would give them the space they both needed to regroup. Maybe the time away would give her the insight she needed on whether to stay or go.

That reminded her—she still needed to inform Evan that she'd be gone. Hopefully he wouldn't tell his questionable friends that her house sat empty. She wanted to be honest with him, wanted him to know that she trusted him, but in all honesty, she didn't. She knew the group he was with was only making his attitude worse, hence his phone call. She had no clue what he truly did with his free time, but she had a feeling it wasn't legal.

Evan had obviously felt himself sinking deeper into a place he didn't want to be when he'd reached out to her. Megan could only pray while she was gone for these two days that the most important men in her life came to some decisions…and she hoped the outcomes would be what she wanted.

"Care to explain what I just saw?"

Cameron winced as he stepped back into his parents' house. Eli stood in the foyer near the sidelight like some Peeping Tom.

"Yeah, I care," Cameron mumbled. The last thing he wanted was to discuss what had just happened because each time he lost his damn mind and kissed Megan, he always felt worse afterward. He was using her to feed his desires, knowing he couldn't go any further.

"Then would you like to tell me why you and Megan look like you're ready to fight one minute and the next thing I know I look out and see you all but devouring her?"

Cameron clenched his fists at his side. Eli's arms crossed over his chest as his eyes narrowed. Eli had married his high school sweetheart, but Megan had been around for so long. And they'd all been friends. *Damn it.* Cameron hadn't even thought of how his brothers would react if they knew…

Hell. Cameron couldn't even put a label on the debacle he'd made of his life in the past month.

"Leave it," Cameron warned as he started down the hall to check on his mom.

"She's resting and Dad's in there." Eli moved quickly, coming to block the entrance to the hall. "I told them we'd lock up and turn off all the lights."

"Fine. You get the lights. I'll check the back door."

Eli made no attempt to move. Raising his gaze to the ceiling, Cameron sighed. He should've known this wasn't going to be easy.

"I have no idea what's going on," he conceded, looking back to his brother. "We've kissed. I know on every level it's a bad idea, but I can't stop myself."

A little of the anger in Eli's eyes dimmed as his shoulders relaxed. "How does she feel?"

Cameron couldn't help but laugh. "Oh, she's made it clear she's ready to step from the friend zone to something more."

Eli tipped his head and shrugged. "And you're angry about this?"

"You know I've made it clear for years I don't want a commitment. Megan's heard me say it over and over." Damn her for making him so confused. "I won't use her, Eli. She's the type of woman who deserves stability and a family. I can't give her either."

"Can't or won't?"

No, he wasn't getting into this. Cameron maneuvered around Eli and went to make sure the back door was locked. When he came back to the front, Eli had turned off the lights except the small lamp on the accent table.

Eli opened the door and gestured for Cameron to

go on ahead. Once they were on the porch, Cameron started to head down the steps, but Eli had to open his mouth again. Ridiculous to think he'd be able to make a break for it.

"You can't be married to your job forever," Eli called out. "At some point you're going to be lonely. Megan's a great girl. You two would be good together."

Cameron spun around. "I'm not looking for advice on my love life. There are complications that you don't know about and I can't get into. So just drop it, and don't mention what you saw to anybody."

Eli stared back, not saying a word.

"Promise me," Cameron demanded. "Not Drake, not Mom or Dad."

After a minute, Eli nodded. "Fine. But you better not mess around and hurt Megan. She's the only woman in your life other than your mother who puts up with your moodiness and your unruly schedule."

Cameron turned back, heading toward his truck parked last in the driveway. He wasn't even entertaining thoughts of how much Megan had put up with. Because then he'd have to admit how much she truly did care for him.

Cameron knew he wasn't going to get any sleep at all tonight, so he headed to the station. Might as well check in with his guys and see if there were any new developments. Of course, if there had been anything, he would've been called. Still, he couldn't go home because Megan's presence was in every single room… especially his bedroom.

His office was practically Megan-free, and he always had work he could do. But Eli was right. Cameron was afraid to go deeper with Megan. How could he be anything else? Too much rested on his shoulders, and no matter what weight he relieved himself of, he'd have more taking its place.

Everything in his life, both personal and professional, all pointed back to Megan somehow. There wasn't a damn thing he could do to save her from his choices, regardless of the path he took.

Chapter Eleven

Megan thought for sure that after visiting the new facility and meeting the staff she'd potentially be working with, she'd have a clearer insight on a decision.

As she maneuvered her car onto the exit ramp that would take her back into Stonerock, she was more confused than ever.

Yes, the facility was beautiful. But the nicest computer equipment or fancy waiting areas, complete with a waterfall wall for a calming atmosphere, weren't going to sway her into making a life-altering decision.

What Megan cared about was the people she'd be able to reach, to help, the difference she could make in their lives. Megan's potential supervisor had gone into great detail about the areas the clinic planned to target. Topping the list were poverty-stricken neighborhoods where alcoholism and drug abuse had spiked in the past few years.

Just the mention of that area had pulled Megan's mind back home with Evan. She knew he had a problem, and she'd give anything to fix him. That's what she did; she had a degree to fix people. But if he didn't want to change completely, she could use all the fancy words and textbook cures in the world and he'd still remain in the pit he'd dug for himself. Though she didn't think he was using drugs—she hadn't seen the telltale signs—she did believe he was mixed up with a group who wasn't immune to the industry. Why else did he always need money? Why else would he always be worried about his safety?

So did she truly want to leave, risking Evan choosing to stay behind? Or did she want to stay in Stonerock where she'd already developed relationships with clients? Those clients trusted her, counted on her. Would they feel as if they were being abandoned if she accepted the new position?

Megan's cell rang, cutting off the radio. Pressing the button on her steering wheel, Megan answered.

"Hello?"

"Hey, Megan." Marly's chipper voice came through the car speakers. "Are you busy?"

"Just driving. What's up?"

"Nora and I were wondering if you were free tonight. I know it's last minute, but Eli said he didn't mind keeping the girls for us."

As exhausted as she was from her whirlwind trip, a girls' night out sounded like the reward she needed.

Megan couldn't remember the last time she'd been out with a group of friends. Going out with Cameron didn't count, not that they went out. They tended to grill at his house or watch movies, and then she'd go back to her house.

"Count me in," Megan said, turning onto her road. "I'm almost home. I need to change, but I can meet you all somewhere."

"We're heading to Dolly's Bar and Grill."

They arranged the time and Megan suddenly found herself getting another burst of energy. She wouldn't think about Evan, Cameron or her work situation. She'd have a beer, chat with the girls and have a good time. A simple, relaxing evening.

With the days losing light earlier and earlier, she too often found herself in pajamas by six o'clock. When had she gotten to that stage in life that the best part of her day was spent in pj's? Mercy, she was getting old.

As soon as Megan examined her closet, she knew she wanted to dress a little sassier than usual tonight. Even if she was just going out with Nora and Marly, Megan had that female urge to step up her game a notch.

When had she let herself get so dowdy and boring? Lately she'd only donned the barest of makeup for work, and she couldn't remember the last time she'd pulled out her curling iron or straightener. If she looked under her bathroom sink, she'd probably find them overtaken by dust.

Glancing at the clock, Megan decided she had time to put some effort into her appearance tonight. After a quick shower, she opted for the big iron and put large, bouncy waves into her hair. A little more shadow than usual made her green eyes pop. Why didn't she do this more often? Just what she'd done so far had boosted both her energy level and confidence.

After pulling on a simple yellow tank-style dress, Megan wrapped a thick belt around her waist, threw on a fitted navy cardigan and pulled on her favorite cowgirl boots. Surely she had earrings that went with this outfit. Digging through her meager stash of jewelry, she managed to find some dangly hoops and a chunky silver bracelet.

Megan grabbed her purse and headed out the door. She hadn't heard from Evan in a couple of days, and, surprisingly, her house hadn't been bothered while she'd been gone.

The guilt of expecting him or his friends to steal something weighed heavily in her gut.

Megan shook off all negative thoughts as she pulled into Dolly's. It being a Friday night, the place was bustling with cars filling the parking lot and people piling in through the front doors.

Music blasted out of the bar as a group of guys held the door open and gestured for her to enter. Smiling her thanks, Megan stepped inside, quickly scanned the room and found Nora and Marly in a booth along the wall.

With a wave, Megan wove her way through the crowd as a slow country song filled the room. Hand in hand, couples made their way to the scarred wooden dance floor. Megan refused to allow the image of her and Cameron dancing to occupy her mind. She was here for fun and for a girls' night. Nothing more.

Nora slid over, giving Megan room to ease onto the leather seat.

"You look beautiful," Nora said with a huge smile. "I was just happy to shower and actually attempt to fix my hair."

Marly laughed. "You're always gorgeous, Nora. But, seriously, Megan, you look great."

"Thanks." Megan sat her purse between her and Nora and thanked God she'd taken some extra time to get ready. "I was going for the fun Megan instead of therapist Megan."

"Well, honey, you nailed it." Nora waved her hand at a waitress. "First round's on me."

"I need a drink," Marly stated. "I've been sewing on Willow's Halloween costume for a week and it still looks like a hot mess. Why the hell did I think I could be supermom instead of just buying one?"

Nora patted Marly's arm. "Because you're an awesome mom and Willow doesn't care what it looks like. She's just excited her mom is making the Darth Vader-cowgirl-princess getup."

Marly moaned. "I suppose. I think letting her pick her favorite themes was a bad idea. I meant one character, not three combined."

Once they ordered their drinks plus a basket of chips and salsa, Megan turned to Nora.

"How's Bev? She getting used to those crutches?" Megan asked.

"Eli said she's still complaining about using them,

but he told her she'd get used to it." Nora rested an elbow on the dull wooden tabletop and smiled. "As long as Mac is there, though, she doesn't have to get up for anything except to use the bathroom. He's right at her side making sure she doesn't even have to ask."

Marly laughed, pushing back a wayward curl from her forehead. "The St. John males have a tendency to go overboard with protecting and assisting their ladies."

Megan thought about how Cameron had wanted her to show Evan some tough love. Cameron was ready to step in and be her human shield, but she had held him back. She remembered a time in high school when a guy was insistent she leave a party with him and all but dragged her toward his car. Cameron had stepped in then, as well, and punched the guy in the face.

The waitress came back with the drinks and each woman took a long, sigh-worthy sip. Megan licked the frothy, fruity foam off her top lip and glanced up to see the other two staring at her.

"What?"

"You were daydreaming." Nora quirked a brow while sliding her fingertip over the condensation on her tall, slender glass. "I know this is absolutely none of my business, but we've known each other a really long time."

Megan braced herself for whatever Nora was about to ask.

"Any chance you and Cameron…" Nora let the silent question settle between them as she pulled the toothpick full of pineapple out of her drink and plucked a piece off.

Marly eased her forearms onto the table and leaned forward, obviously eager to hear the answer, as well.

Megan shrugged. "We're best friends." That was the truth. "I'm not sure we would know how to be anything else."

"Have you tried?" Marly asked.

The waitress returned, setting a giant basket of tortilla chips and three small bowls of salsa on the table.

Megan pretended to look for the perfect chip while she contemplated the answer she should give over the answer she wanted to give.

"I believe the silence speaks for itself," Nora proudly stated as she dipped her chip. "There's no way a man like Cameron can ignore you for years."

Yeah, well, he had. At least in any form beyond friendship. But when his mouth had been on hers, his hands up her shirt, he'd certainly given off the vibe he was staking a claim.

"How long have you guys been a secret?" Nora asked, leaning in just a bit more, a wide, knowing smile spread across her face.

Megan sighed. "There's no secret. To be honest, we only kissed for the first time last week and that was because I was sleeping, he startled me from a dream and I…"

"Please, please don't stop there." Marly reached across and squeezed her arm. "I may not have known you that long, but I'm wrapped up in this and I know it's not my business. So, tell Nora and just let me listen in."

Megan laughed and took a drink, welcoming the chill of the strawberry-flavored, alcohol-enriched slush. "I yanked him down and kissed him," she muttered.

Both women's eyes widened as their grins spread even wider. Megan couldn't help but smile back because she so had to get this off her chest. And there wasn't a doubt in her mind these two ladies would offer her some much-needed advice.

"Then he cornered me in his kitchen the other night after we watched your kids during your date." Megan found herself moving forward with the story without being prompted. She wanted to blame the alcohol, but after only two sips, that defense fell flat. "He was angry at the kiss we'd shared."

"If he cornered you and was angry, sounds to me like he's turned on and is mad at himself," Nora supplied. "Probably for just now taking notice, if you ask me."

"Yeah, well, we argued. That led to another kiss and his hand up my shirt."

Nora and Marly high-fived each other across the table, and Megan felt her face flush. "This is silly." She laughed. "I feel like I'm in high school."

"Better than high school," Marly chimed in. "Way better. So what happened next? This is the best girls' night ever."

Megan reached for another chip. "Sorry to disappoint, but he pulled back and we argued again. I just don't know what to do."

Nora shifted in her seat and all smiling vanished as she looked Megan straight in the eyes. "Take my advice. Don't wait to tell him how you feel, what you truly want. I did that with Eli the first time. We let a lot of years and hurt build between us, and then we had to overcome so much to be together. You're not guaranteed a tomorrow."

Megan felt the quick sting in her nose as her eyes started to fill. Nora had been in love with Eli in school, and then he had gone into the military. After a few years, Nora married Eli's friend, who had ultimately died while deployed. Nora had taken the long, hard road to find love, and Megan could only nod as the lump formed in her throat.

"Damn it." Marly yanked her napkin from under her drink and dabbed beneath her eyes. "I had my makeup so nice, too, thanks to that pin I saw on Pinterest."

"I didn't mean to cause tears," Nora defended herself, passing another napkin over to Marly. "I'm just trying to help."

Megan blinked back her own unshed tears and gripped her icy-cold glass. "You did help. I know I need to tell him how I feel, but I guess I just needed encouragement. I'm a bit of a coward. What if we mess up? He's the most stable person in my life, and I can't lose him as a best friend."

Nora nodded. "I understand the fear, but if he loves you beyond friends, isn't that worth the risk? Is he worth it?"

Without a doubt. Cameron was worth risking everything for.

Her phone chimed from her purse. She thought it was rude to be on the phone when out with a group of people, but it could be a patient in need.

"Sorry," she said, digging out the phone. "Give me one second."

The caller ID flashed her brother's name. Megan swiped the screen and answered.

"Evan?"

"I'm ready."

Those two words held so much meaning. "You want me to come and get you?"

"Yeah, um, I was dropped off at the parking lot beside the old gas station that closed. You know where that's at?"

Megan nodded, even though he couldn't see her. "Yes. I'll be there in five minutes."

She hung up, quickly pulled money from her purse and tossed it on the table before explaining to the girls that she had to get her brother. There was no time to go into further details because Evan changed his mind so often, she wanted to jump through this window of opportunity.

Besides, he might be in danger if he was in a parking lot at night all alone.

Megan raced for her SUV. As she pulled into the lot, at first she didn't see anybody. As soon as she got out, she felt the presence of someone behind her. Spinning around, her heart leaped into her throat. The hulking figure wasn't Evan.

Pulling all her experience and courage to the surface, Megan lifted her chin and squared her shoulders. "Where's my brother?" she asked.

The sneer on the stranger's face sent a cold chill down her spine. He stepped closer, all the while raking his eyes over her. Curse this dress she'd felt beautiful in earlier. Why was she now feeling as if she was being punished for wanting to look nice?

"I'm right here."

Megan jerked around to see Evan, hands in his pockets, staring across the open space. She could barely see him for the glow from the streetlight that was at the other end of the block. But the tone of his voice worried her. He sounded sad, nervous, almost desperate.

"What's going on?" she asked Evan as she started to take a step forward.

The man behind her gripped her arm. Megan had taken a self-defense course, a requirement for her job. Instantly the lessons came flooding to her mind. She whirled around and shoved the palm of her free hand straight up into the man's nose.

With a howl, he dropped her arm and covered his face. She shook out her wrist and glanced over her shoulder to Evan.

"Get in my car," she ordered, her gaze volleying back and forth between her brother and the man who would no doubt be angry. She didn't want to be there when he decided to retaliate. "Now, Evan."

"I can't."

Another man seemed to materialize behind Evan. This man held a gun...pointed at her. The hulk behind her gripped her arm once again, this time tighter as he yanked her back against his chest.

"They'll kill us if we don't do what they want," Evan told her. "I had no clue they were setting me up, Meg. I'm sorry."

Apologies could wait. Right now she needed to figure out how to get them out of here without getting shot. "What do you want?" she asked, still trying to keep her voice calm though she was anything but.

"Your brother here owes us twenty thousand dollars," the man behind her stated, his hot breath against her cheek making her gag. "And after that stunt you just pulled on me, I'm adding another five K."

Why hadn't she paid more attention to her brother? Whatever mess he'd gotten wrapped up in had apparently been going on awhile if he owed that kind of money. Still, all that could be dealt with later. Right now she needed to figure out a way to survive the night. She wanted Cameron. He wouldn't be afraid; he would arrest these guys and save her and Evan. But Cameron wasn't here, and she'd have to fend for herself.

"I'm sure you know I don't have that much money on me," she told them, her eyes darting to the gun still aimed at her.

Sirens filled the night, and Megan nearly wept with relief. She forced herself to keep in mind her surroundings and the men who were threatening her. She may not be a cop like Cameron, but she'd counseled enough addicts to know that if they were high, they didn't care who they hurt. They had nothing to lose. Which meant she was expendable.

Before she knew it, the man behind her let go, causing her to stumble back from the force of his departure. The man with the gun patted Evan on the shoulder as if they were the best of friends.

"Come on, man." The guy shoved his gun in his waistband. "You ain't waiting to talk to no cops. You're with us till you pay up."

Evan threw her one last pained look and mouthed "sorry" before turning and running off into the night with the men who'd just threatened their lives. With shaky knees and tremors overtaking her body, Megan sank to the cool concrete. Moments later, a cruiser pulled in, too late to save her brother.

Chapter Twelve

Never in his life had fear crippled him to the point of losing control and being ready to throw it all away.

But the sight of Megan in the clutches of notorious gang leader "The Shark" was an image that would haunt him forever.

Then the gun had appeared, and Cameron had to get a patrol car sounding that second. He knew those guys. He knew they wouldn't shoot Megan unless provoked. The siren did its job and the criminals fled—including her lowlife brother. Cameron wanted to get ahold of that man and punch him in the face for not protecting his sister.

What the hell had Megan been doing there, anyway? His heart had nearly exploded in his chest when he saw her black SUV pull into the lot. He'd gotten a good look at her sexy little dress and cowgirl boots, showcasing those shapely legs. But even that punch of lust had vanished the second those dangerous thugs had surrounded her.

Now, an hour later, Cameron stood on her porch. He knew she was inside because his officer had told him he'd driven Megan's car home while another officer drove her in his cruiser. She was too shaken up, too scared to drive.

Cameron slid his key into her lock and let himself in. The second he stepped over the threshold, he called her name, not wanting to alarm her because he'd come in the front door and not the back as he normally did.

He heard the sound of her boots clicking over the wooden floor from the rear of the house. Megan came down the hallway, her arms wrapped around her midsection, her face pale.

For her fear alone he vowed to get enough evidence on these guys to put them away for a long, long time. Right now, though, he wished he wasn't on the right side of the law. He wished more than anything he could track them down and beat them within an inch of their lives, forgetting about the justice system altogether and saving the taxpayers' dollars.

"I knew they'd call you." She pasted on a smile that fell short of convincing. "Did they find Evan? I've texted and called him, but…"

Fury threatened to take over. She was worried about Evan? After a man had held her at gunpoint while another practically held her captive?

"My officers were more concerned with you." Only

because the FBI was still out there right now keeping an eye on the traffickers…and because Cameron had told his two officers to make sure Megan was watched until he arrived. "Evan is a big boy."

Anything else he said would be out of anger, and the last thing he wanted to do was fight. Between the way her vulnerability had settled between them like a third party and the way that dress hugged her body, Cameron was having a really difficult time prioritizing his emotions.

"Are you okay?" he asked, taking a step forward, then another, until he was within reaching distance. But he fisted his hands at his side. "My officers told me you weren't hurt, but I needed to hear it from you. I needed to see you."

Those bright green eyes seemed even more vibrant than usual. Cameron didn't know if he was just now noticing or if she'd done something tricky with her makeup. Regardless, the way she watched him, the way she seemed to be holding herself back, had him nearing the breaking point. He'd been holding on by the proverbial thread for so long now; it was only a matter of time before he fell.

Megan reached up, shoved her hair back from her face. "I'm fine."

Her action drew his gaze to her arm, to the fingerprint-size bruises dotting her perfect skin. Cameron clenched his teeth, reining in his anger because none of this was her fault and he wouldn't make her the target simply because she was the only one here once the rage fully surfaced. The only thing he could fault Megan with was having a kind heart and wanting to help people who would continue to stomp on her and use her.

Cameron gripped her wrist in one hand and slid a fingertip from his other over around the marred skin. "You're not fine. This never should've happened."

He'd cursed himself for standing by and watching as events unfolded, but had he gone charging for her as he'd wanted to, as his heart told him to, his cover would've been blown and she would have known the cops were watching Evan. *Cameron* was watching Evan.

That heavy ball of guilt was something he'd have to live with. If there had ever been any doubt before, tonight just proved that he would choose his job first every single time. He hated himself for it, but that's how he was made up.

"They're just bruises," she whispered, her eyes still on his.

Goose bumps raised beneath his fingertips as he continued to stroke her skin. "I don't like them."

Megan placed a hand over his, halting his movement. Her lids closed as she whispered, "Please, Cam. I just…"

Bowing her head, Megan sighed.

"You what, baby?"

"I wanted you to come," she muttered beneath the curtain of her hair that had cascaded around her face. "I wanted you here because I knew I'd feel safe. But now that you're here, I can't let you touch me." Slowly lifting her head, she brought her eyes up to lock on to his. "It makes me want things. Want you."

Damn it. There went that last thread he'd been holding on to.

Cameron stepped into her, trapping their hands between their bodies. The tip of his nose brushed against hers, leaving their mouths barely a whisper apart.

"You are always safe with me," he told her, slowly moving his lips across hers with the lightest of touches. "And tonight you're mine."

"Just tonight," she agreed. "We don't need to put a label on it, and I don't want to think beyond now."

Cameron captured her mouth, completely ignoring all the warnings pounding through his head. Totally shoving aside all the reasons this was a terrible idea: the investigation, the risk of losing his best friend and the fact he'd just admitted to himself that his job would always come first. All that mattered was Megan and this ache he'd had for her for years. It wasn't going away no matter how noble he tried to be. His hormones didn't give a damn about his morals or standards.

Megan's mouth opened beneath his as she tried to pull her hands free. Cameron was quicker, holding them firm as he broke from the kiss.

"You're mine," he repeated, nipping her lips, her chin, trailing a line down to her collarbone. "I don't know why you have on this dress with these boots, but it's driving me crazy. Tell me you weren't on a date earlier."

Tipping her head back, arching into him, Megan let out one of those sweet moans he was starting to love. "No, no date," she panted. "I was out with Nora and Marly."

The fact she was out with his sisters-in-law thrilled him because if she'd been out with a guy, Cameron would've had to admit jealousy.

Cameron released her hands and slid his palms over her curvy hips. He gripped her and pulled her pelvis flush with his as he continued to rain kisses along her exposed skin just above the dip in her dress. Just above the perfect swell of her breasts.

Megan wrapped her delicate fingers around his biceps and squeezed as he yanked down the top of her dress. Material tore, but he didn't care. He'd buy her a new one.

"Cam."

He froze at her plea. "Meg, I'm sorry. After what you went through tonight, I wasn't thinking."

Her lips curved into a smile. "I wasn't complaining. I know you'd never hurt me."

Seeing her lips swollen from his kisses, her neck and the tops of her breasts pink from arousal, an instant flood of possessiveness filled him. The only mark he ever wanted on her was from him, from passion.

"If you keep this up, I don't know how much longer I can stand." Her arms slid around his neck as she rubbed her body against his. "You make my knees weak and we're still fully clothed."

"I'm about to fix that problem."

He unbuckled her belt and let it drop with a clatter to the wood floor. He gripped the hem of her dress, yanked it up and over her head, then tossed the unwanted garment aside.

The sight of her standing before him wearing a pale pink bra and matching panties along with those cowgirl boots was enough to make his own knees weak.

Megan reached for his shirt, but he pulled it off before she could touch him. In record time their clothes were mere puddles on the floor. From the way her eyes kept sampling him, Cameron knew if he didn't try to keep some sort of control, this night would be over before he could truly enjoy it.

"I've waited to see you look at me like that," Megan told him, rising up on her toes to kiss his jawline. "Like you really want me."

She was killing him. With the way the lace from her bra pressed against his bare skin, her raw, honest words and the delicate way her mouth cruised over him, Megan was gradually overpowering him.

Gliding his hands around her curves, Cameron lifted her until her legs went around his waist. The leather from her cowgirl boots rubbed his back, but the fact he finally had this woman wrapped all over him overrode his discomfort.

"I'm too heavy for you," she argued, nipping at his ear.

Palming her backside, his thumb teased the edge of her lacy panty line. "Baby, you're the perfect weight for me," he growled as he headed toward the living room and the L-shaped sofa. "Absolutely perfect."

Without easing his hold, Cameron settled her onto

the corner of the couch as his lips took hold of hers once again. He could kiss her forever.

Too bad he couldn't do forever. Selfishly, he was doing now, tonight, and he'd hate himself later for taking advantage even if she had given him the green light.

Megan's legs fell away from his waist, her boots landing on either side of his feet. Cameron eased back, picked up one leg at a time and pried off her cowgirl boots. She watched him beneath heavy lids, her chest rising and falling as she licked her lips in anticipation.

Coming to his full height, Cameron stared down at this magnificent woman practically laid out for him. His throat grew tight with emotions...emotions he could certainly identify but he couldn't allow to take over.

"You're stunning," he told her, completely taking in the display.

Without a word, Megan sat up, reached behind and unfastened her bra. After sliding it down her arms and tossing it to the side, she hooked her thumbs beneath her panties and slid them down, never once taking her eyes off his. The minor striptease was the most erotic moment of his life, and it had lasted all of ten seconds. Megan had a power over him that no other woman could match.

"Tell me you have protection," she whispered as she reached for him. Flat palms slid up over his chest and around his neck.

Cameron allowed her to pull him down, and he loved the feel of her beneath him. He had to remind himself not to get used to this, not to want this ever again.

"I don't have anything." One fingertip slid up and over her breast. "But I'm clean. I have regular physicals for work and I've always used protection. It's your call."

"I'm clean, too, and I've always been protected." Megan smiled, wrapping her legs around Cameron's narrow waist once again. "So what are we waiting for?"

The darkness that had settled into Cameron's blue eyes revealed so much. Who knew her best friend had a possessive streak when it came to intimacy? The way he held her, spoke to her, dominated her, thrilled Megan in a way she'd never before experienced and she knew without a doubt that this was it for her... *He* was it for her. No other man would compare with Cameron St. John.

She wanted to lose herself in him, wanted to forget all the ugliness and worries in her life. She wanted him to show her how beautiful they could be together because her fantasy had already paled in comparison.

"Tell me what you want," he murmured against her lips.

She trembled beneath his touch. No, that wasn't her. Cameron's hands were shaking as he slid them over her breasts.

Framing his face with her hands, she held his gaze. "You're nervous." She didn't ask and she wasn't making fun of him.

Cameron closed his eyes, resting his forehead against hers. "Nobody else has ever mattered this much."

Megan didn't know what to say to that revealing piece of information, so she tucked it in the back of her mind. Stroking his bottom lip with her thumb, she kept her eyes on his.

"I want anything you're willing to give," she said, answering his earlier question. "Anything you want to do."

A low groan escaped him. Then, as if some invisible barrier broke, Cameron consumed her. His hands took journeys all over her body, leaving goose bumps in their wake. That talented mouth demanded kisses, demanded passion.

Cameron settled himself between her legs, gliding one hand down her quivering abdomen to cup her most aching area. Megan tilted her hips, ready to burst for just one simple touch. She was officially at his mercy.

Easing his hand away, he held on to her waist. "Look at me," he demanded. "Only me."

"Only you."

As he slid into her, Megan gasped. Every dream, every waking fantasy she'd ever had about her best friend, didn't prepare her for the onslaught of emotions, waves of pleasure and such an awakening. They moved together as if they'd been made for each other, as if their bodies automatically knew how to respond to each other.

Cameron's arms wrapped around her as he lifted her off the couch. Still connected, he turned and sat, leaving her to straddle him...surrendering all power and control to Megan.

In that moment, she knew he loved her. He may not say it, he may not want to face the fact, but there was no way this man could look at her, make love to her, as if she were the only woman in the world and not love her.

Ripples of pleasure began to build, each one stronger than the last. Megan wanted to be fully fused with him when her body flew apart. Gripping his shoulders, she leaned down and claimed his mouth. Seconds later spasms took hold. With one hand firmly against the small of her back and the other cupping the nape of her neck, Cameron held her tight against his body as he stilled and trembled right along with her.

Moments after they fell over the edge together, Cameron still held on to her, still commanded her lips. The man wasn't done just because his body had hit the finish line.

His tongue slid along her bottom lip, his kisses softer, shorter…as if he didn't want this moment to end. At least, that's how she hoped he felt.

"Stay with me," she muttered around his kisses. "In my bed. Just for tonight."

His darkened, heavy-lidded gaze met hers. She thought for sure he'd deny her—they'd only agreed on this one time—but she had to ask. She wasn't ready to let him go.

Circling his arms tighter around her waist, Cameron came to his feet. Megan's legs instinctively wrapped around him.

"You seem to like my legs here," she joked, hoping to break the tension because he still hadn't answered her.

He headed out into the hall and toward her bedroom. "I intend to keep them here."

Chapter Thirteen

He'd guaranteed nothing beyond that night. Hadn't promised pretty words or a happily-ever-after. Megan had known exactly what she was getting into with him. He'd made his intentions perfectly clear before he'd peeled her out of her clothes.

So why did he feel like a jerk for leaving her before she woke?

Because he was.

Cameron sat on his deck, looking out over the pond as the morning sun reflected off the water. He didn't take time out here anymore, didn't just relax and enjoy life.

Last night he'd enjoyed life to the absolute fullest, which only made him want more. But his career didn't mesh well with a personal life. He couldn't compartmentalize and keep things separated, neat and orderly anymore. But he wanted Megan in one area, the friend area. He wanted her far away from anything that could harm her, like her useless brother who hadn't been able to protect her last night.

Cameron cursed, propping his bare feet up on the rail. He hadn't been able to protect her, either. Apparently he was no better than Evan at this point.

Opting to beat himself up over how everything went down last night was better than rehashing all that could have gone wrong in those few seconds. It also kept his mind off what had happened afterward.

Okay, so that was a lie. Even Cameron couldn't pretend to be unfazed by what had happened at Megan's house. How could he forget how perfectly they'd come together? How she'd clung to him? He could practically still feel her breath on his cheek, feel her curvy body beneath his hands. Those sighs of pleasure tickling his ear and the way she called his name on a groan were locked so deep in to his soul, he knew forgetting the intimacy they'd shared was impossible.

Closing his eyes, Cameron clenched his fists on the arms of his Adirondack chair. He hadn't given a thought to what would happen after he'd made love to Megan. Hadn't cared about feelings or excuses after the fact. All Cameron had wanted was to feel her, consume her. The fantasy come to life had been his only focus, and now here he sat with a sated body and a guilty conscience.

Between his ever-evolving feelings and the worry he'd seen in her eyes when he'd arrived at her house,

Cameron had told himself he was there to console her. That was a flat-out lie. He'd needed to comfort himself because he'd been a trembling mess.

Now his priority was to check in with the station, where some of the FBI agents had set up temporary headquarters until this case was over. He knew if something major had happened, he would have been notified. Still, as the chief, he needed to check in and get an update.

His cell vibrated in his pocket. Dropping his feet to the deck floor, he slid the phone out and read the screen.

I didn't take you for a coward

The harsh words hit right where Megan intended... his heart. Her text couldn't have been more accurate. He was a coward, and she'd called him out. One of the things he loved about her was her ability to never back down.

He honestly had no clue how to reply, and this wasn't a conversation to be had via text. He wouldn't be that guy and he sure as hell would treat Megan with more respect. The thought was laughable, considering he'd done the walk of shame out her back door, but he would make it up to her. Somehow.

Ignoring the text wasn't an option, either. Cameron quickly replied.

Be at my place at noon

That would give him time to check in with the station, figure out where the hell Evan was and grab a quick shower. Cameron planned to have a little talk with Evan. Cameron had to play every scenario out in his head because he couldn't tip off the guy. But he had every intention of making it clear that dragging Megan into his illegal mess was unacceptable and intolerable.

The phone vibrated in his hand.

If I have time

Smiling, Cameron came to his feet. She'd be there. He was sure of it. If she wasn't, then he'd find her. They weren't done. Not by a long shot.

Now he just had to figure out what the hell to do with his feelings and how to eliminate the possibility of hurting hers. Because, damn it, he still wanted her. Wanted Megan with a passion that went beyond all they'd shared last night. How could he tell her that and still try to keep her at a distance? How could he even try to take a chance with her but keep her safe and away from his job?

Granted, he worked in a small town and the crime rate, for the most part, was low. But there were instances that crept up, and he was the man to take control. He couldn't have his life both ways, and the decision ate at him because he knew he'd have to give up something—or someone—he loved.

Cameron headed inside to make a few calls. First things first. Right now he needed to find Evan and have a man-to-man talk. Then he'd deal with Megan.

If Cameron St. John thought he could turn her world inside out with a few orgasms, leave without a word and then have the nerve to summon her to his house, he truly didn't know her.

Megan took a deep breath, counted backward from ten and mounted the steps to Mac and Bev's house. She hadn't seen Cameron's truck in the drive or along the street, so she figured now would be a good time to stop and check on Bev. No doubt the woman was fed up with St. John testosterone ordering her to stay put while they did everything for her.

Megan didn't want to go in all angry and frustrated because then she'd have to explain. There was absolutely no way she'd be revealing to Cameron's parents why she was a bit irritable this morning.

After ringing the doorbell, Megan stepped back and waited. Mac pulled the door open, sending the fall floral wreath swaying against the glass.

"Megan." Mac extended his hand, taking hers and pulling her into the foyer. "I'm so glad to see you."

Laughing, Megan allowed herself to be ushered in. "Wow, I've never had such a lovely greeting before."

"I think Bev hates me," he whispered. "She just threatened to bash me with her crutch if I asked her one more time if she needed anything."

Megan patted Mac's arm and smiled. "I'm sure the threat was out of love."

Glancing toward the living room, Mac shook his head. "I doubt it," he said, turning back to her. "If you're going to be a few minutes, would you mind if I ran out to the hardware store? I hate to leave her even though she's told me to go."

Megan nodded. "You go on. We'll be just fine."

Mac seemed to breathe a sigh of relief as his shoulders relaxed. "Thanks, Megan. I'll only be twenty minutes, at the most."

"Take your time."

Mac eased around her, grabbed his keys from the table and headed out the door. Still amused at the fear in Mac's eyes, Megan headed to the living room, where Bev had her feet propped up on the footrest of the recliner. Some cooking channel was muted on the TV.

"Thank God he's gone," Bev said as soon as Megan stepped into the room. "That man needs to stop hovering."

Megan sank onto the edge of the old sofa, angling her body to face Bev. "He just loves you."

Bev dropped the remote into her lap. "I know. I keep telling myself that, but it's a broken ankle. I'm not dying."

Megan glanced around the walls at all the years of memories, family vacations and military medals adorning the space. This family was full of love, full of life and always so supportive.

She couldn't help but wonder what her life would've been like had her parents survived. What would her brother's life have been like? Would he still have felt that urge to rebel at every single thing? "You okay, honey?"

Glancing back to Bev, Megan nodded, swallowing the lump of emotions threatening to clog her throat. "I've been better," Megan answered honestly. "But I came to check on you, not discuss me."

Bev waved a hand. "Oh, please. Everyone has checked on me. I'm fine. What's got you so worried?"

There was no way Megan would get into all the issues that swirled around in her mind. Whatever she and Cameron had going on—or not going on—would remain between them. She had no label for it, had no way of knowing where the next step would take them.

Bev knew enough about Evan, though, that Megan found herself opening up about him. She explained what happened the night before, stopping at the point where Cameron ended up staying the night. Megan had been around this family for so long, Bev had seen Evan's downfall, witnessed Megan's frustration.

"As a woman who raised three hellions, let me tell you that you can only do so much." Bev shifted in her chair until she could reach out and take Megan's hand in hers. "You guide them the best way you can, but in the end they have to make their own decisions."

These were all facts Megan knew, but she still ached for a peace she may never find with her only living relative.

"Those were your kids. It's a bit different with Evan because he's always quick to throw in my face how I'm not his mother." Megan smiled and shrugged. "Besides, your boys all turned out perfect."

Bev's laughter filled the cozy living room. "Oh, honey. They're far from perfect. I had a full head of gray hair by the time I was thirty-five. I swore I wouldn't make it through their teen years without getting a call from the cops about one or all three. They seemed to travel in a pack."

Megan couldn't help but laugh herself. "Yeah, they got me drunk during my senior prom."

"Oh, mercy," Bev whispered, shaking her head. "I think I'm better off not knowing some of the things they did. I cringe just thinking of the stuff I know about."

Megan took comfort in Bev's gentle hand. So many times she'd wanted motherly advice and she'd always known she could turn to Bev at any time. Unfortunately, with the Cameron situation, Megan wasn't about to seek support. She'd have to figure out that one all on her own.

"Evan wouldn't keep in contact with you if he didn't love you," Bev went on. "He may take some time, but you're the only stable person in his life. He'll come back to you."

Megan squeezed Bev's hand. "I hope so."

Because even though she didn't have concrete evidence of his extracurricular activities, she wasn't stupid. If he didn't change his ways, the end result would be either jail or death. Megan didn't know if she had the strength to get through either of those.

Cameron kept his voice low, his back to the brick building, so he could keep an eye on the open end of the alley. He'd found out Evan was in the shady part of a neighboring town, just outside Cameron's jurisdiction.

After throwing on a ball cap and sunglasses, Cameron had gone into the pool hall and firmly told Evan to meet him out back.

Now the coward had the nerve to look worried.

"Maybe you should've been a little more concerned last night for your sister." It took every ounce of Cameron's self-control to keep him from pummeling Megan's brother. "Do you have any idea how scared she was? You may run with these guys, but she doesn't, and she has a heart of gold. You realize that afterward she was more worried about you than what could've happened to her?"

Evan glanced away, but Cameron wasn't having it. Cameron smacked his cheek. "Look at me. Megan said one of your so-called friends had a gun on her. Do you want to see your sister wrapped up in this mess you're in? Do you want to see her hurt or worse?"

Something flared in Evan's eyes. Anger, hatred, who knew what, but at least there was some sign that he actually cared about Megan.

"You have no idea what's going on in my life," Evan spat.

Cameron didn't react, didn't say a word. No sense in giving away that he in fact knew nearly everything that was going on. Knew so much that warrants were about to be processed for the arrest of two major players in the drug-running ring and for Evan, though Evan's charges weren't as harsh. Still, Cameron wanted the charges to stick. He wanted Evan to hit rock bottom so he'd get the help he needed and maybe eventually be the brother Megan deserved.

Disgusted that he was getting nowhere, Cameron started to turn away. "Keep her safe." Evan's low, pleading words froze Cameron in his tracks.

Glancing over his shoulder, Cameron met Evan's

eyes and for the first time he actually saw a man who showed genuine concern and fear for someone other than himself. "She doesn't have anybody else," Evan stated, still holding Cameron's gaze.

Cameron nodded. "Whose fault is that?"

When Evan continued to stare, as if waiting for affirmation, Cameron replied, "I won't let anything happen to her."

As he walked away and headed back toward his truck, he wondered if he'd just lied. Could he honestly keep Megan from getting hurt? Oh, he could prevent her from physical harm, but what about her heart?

The mental scars from this entire scenario would live with her forever. She'd blame herself; she'd question every decision she ever made where her brother was concerned. And she'd hate Cameron.

He slid behind the wheel and brought the engine to life. The clock on his dash showed only thirty minutes until she was due at his house. Knowing Megan, she'd keep him waiting out of spite—which was fine. He needed the extra time to calm down from seeing Evan, from realizing that so much was about to come to a head. All Cameron could do was sit back and proceed with his job...just like always.

Chapter Fourteen

So what if it was nearly two o'clock? Megan wished she could chalk up her tardiness to stubbornness or even the fact she'd been visiting with Bev and Mac. In reality, she'd stuck around with Bev out of nerves.

What would she and Cameron discuss? How did they jump from best friends to the most intimate experience of her life to her waking up alone? Did he really think they would just pal up, watch a movie, grill a steak and hang like they always did on their days off?

Only one way to find out.

Megan mounted the steps and raised her hand to knock. She'd never knocked before. Letting out a sigh, she opened the screen door and twisted the knob on the old oak door. She wouldn't put it past Cameron to lock it since she was late, but the knob turned beneath her palm.

She stepped over the threshold, nerves swirling in her stomach as the familiar scent of Cameron's masculine aroma surrounded her. She'd inhaled that woodsy scent when her face had been pressed into his neck as he'd lowered her into her bed. Never again could she breathe in Cameron's signature scent and not instantly be taken to the time when he'd fulfilled her every desire, her every wish.

Closing the door at her back, Megan sat her purse and keys on the built-in bookshelf to the left of the doorway. The same place she always sat her things when she came in, as if this were her home, too.

Silly thought, really. They'd slept together, not exchanged rings or vows.

A part of Megan wouldn't mind doing just that, but she wouldn't beg any man to love her. Either Cameron would want the same things she did or he wouldn't. No matter how this next phase played out, Megan was a big girl and she'd survive.

But even knowing they'd taken another step deeper into their relationship, Megan still didn't know what to do about the job in Memphis. Being with Cameron was more important than any position she could ever have. She'd give up her dream job in order to have a life with him, but was that something she could convince him of?

She didn't want to have to convince him, though. Megan wanted Cam to come to the realization they belonged together.

And if he didn't, Megan knew she'd have to make

the move because she couldn't live here, see him every day and act as if her heart wasn't shattered.

Heavy footsteps sounded from overhead. Megan glanced toward the stairs just as Cameron came down the first set, then stopped on the landing. His piercing blue eyes held hers as she remained by the door.

"Contemplating whether to stay or go?" he asked.

Shoving her hands in the pockets of her favorite pair of faded jeans, Megan tipped her head. "I don't run away."

Cameron rested his hand on the newel post as he continued to stare down at her. What was he thinking? And why did he look even sexier today now that they'd been intimate?

Keeping his eyes on hers, Cameron slid his hand down the banister as he descended the steps. Megan didn't move, didn't glance away even though her heart was pounding so hard. Cameron came to stand directly in front of her. The way he towered over her had Megan tipping her head back to hold his gaze. Nowhere did he touch her, yet his demanding presence commanded her body to react.

Cameron leaned forward, his lips by her ear. "Don't call me a coward again," he growled.

Pleased he was just as affected by their predicament as she was, Megan forced herself to remain still, to not reach for him and cling as she desperately wanted to. And that was the problem wrapped in the proverbial nutshell. She was desperate for this man's touch, his passion.

When Cameron eased back, just enough for a sliver

of sunlight from the windows to pass through, Megan smiled.

"Hit a nerve, did I?"

"You knew you would."

"Maybe."

Was he just going to stand within a breath of her and not touch her? Maybe he wasn't as affected by their connection as she'd thought. Or perhaps he was into torturing her.

"What's the protocol here, Cam?" she asked, unable to stand the tension for another second. Someone had to step up and start this conversation. "What happens now?"

"What do you want to happen?" he countered.

Megan pulled in a deep breath, knowing full well she walked on a tightrope. "I think I've made things pretty clear. It's you who seems to be torn about what you want."

The muscle in his jaw jumped. He gripped her wrists with one hand, tugging them over her head, causing her to lean back against the door. He trailed his other hand down her arm until she trembled, all the while keeping his eyes locked on hers. She held her breath, unable to fully comprehend the power he had over her and the helpless state she was currently in.

"I'm not torn," he corrected as he brought his palm up to cup her cheek, his thumb stroking her lips. "I know exactly what I want."

That low, sultry tone of his made her body hum with anticipation. Or maybe she was still shaking from the simple touch of his fingertips. Perhaps every single thing about the man made her tingle now that she had let her guard down.

His eyes held hers. "What I want and what is possible are two different things."

It took a moment for the words to register. Megan made to pull his hands away, shaking her head. "That makes no sense," she all but shouted. "You're an adult. You pretty much decide what you want. Do you not want me? I can handle it if that's the case."

Okay, she might not handle it very well, but she would move on. She wasn't playing around anymore.

"I'd say after last night it's obvious I want you."

"Nothing is obvious," she hissed, hating how she still was held captive by him. "I have no clue what's going on with you, Cam. What are you fighting against?"

Cameron opened his mouth as if to say something, but then he shut it. Glancing toward the ground, he muttered a curse as he rubbed the back of his neck and released his hold on her.

He was battling some inner turmoil. Whatever it was, he wasn't opening up about it. The fact he was keeping something that obviously involved her locked inside had Megan hurting in a way she hadn't known possible.

"You know what, forget it." She sighed, throwing her hands in the air. "We'll go back to being friends. We'll chalk last night up to a—"

His eyes narrowed in on her. "Don't say mistake."

"An amazing experience," she finished slowly. "I

won't call it a mistake. What we shared can't be labeled as a mistake. But it won't happen again."

When he merely nodded, a portion of the hope she'd been clinging to died. He offered nothing but that simple gesture of agreement, as if his entire life hadn't changed after the intimacy they'd shared.

Seeing as how he was not much into conversation today, Megan turned toward the built-in and grabbed her keys and purse. In an instant, Cameron's hands covered hers, his body was plastered to her back, his arms stretched out with hers.

"Don't go," he whispered in her ear.

Closing her eyes, Megan dropped her head between her shoulders. "Why did you tell me to come?"

"I wanted to see you." He nuzzled his way through her hair, his lips barely brushing against the side of her neck. "I had no clue what I'd do once you got here. I told myself to keep the friendship above my desire for you. But I can't."

His fingers laced through hers as he placed open-mouthed kisses over the side of her neck and down onto her shoulder. Megan didn't want to respond, wanted to make him work for it, but her head tipped to the side before she could even think.

"I don't know what the hell to do here, Meg."

So much tension radiated from him. She wanted to turn, to hold him and comfort him. Whatever war he waged with himself was something he felt he needed to face alone.

"I've fought this for so long," he went on as his lips continued to travel over her heated skin. "I never wanted to cross this line with you because I knew once I had you, it wouldn't be nearly enough."

Well, that certainly sounded promising.

"Then why do you sound so upset?" she asked, trying to focus on his unspoken problem and not the way he was setting her body on fire with each simple touch of those talented lips.

"I've always said I won't get involved." His fingers tightened around hers, balling their joined hands into fists. "I'm married to this job. The stress, the worry, I wouldn't put that on anybody, least of all you."

Everything always came down his job. She loved how noble he was, but, damn it, he was a man, too. A man with needs, desires. And he was ready to shove it all aside for the sake of his badge?

"I don't mind," she answered honestly. "Maybe you wouldn't feel so stressed if you had someone to share the burden with."

"I can't," he muttered, resting his forehead on her shoulder. "You don't understand."

She started to turn, but he held her away. "Damn it, let me look at you," she cried.

Finally he eased back, releasing her hands. When Megan fully turned to face him, angst and torment stared back at her. She'd never thought she'd see a day when Cameron St. John seemed anything but strong and resilient.

They needed to get off this emotional roller coaster. They needed to return to familiar territory where they weren't so wrapped up in what the next step should be. If that step happened to be in opposite directions, then so be it. But they couldn't lose sight of what was important.

Megan slid a fingertip along the worry lines between Cameron's indrawn brows. "We need a break. *You* need a break." Smiling, she dropped her hand. "I have the perfect idea. Don't go anywhere. I'll be back in thirty minutes to pick you up."

His eyes narrowed. "What do you have in mind?"

"Oh, please." She laughed. "After the shenanigans you and your brothers got into, you're afraid of me?"

His gaze darted to her lips, then back up. "More than you know," he whispered.

How could her body continually respond to his words, his tone and those heated looks? How much did she have to endure before she was put out of her misery and he either moved forward or stepped away? In all honesty, she was done playing. So she was going after all she wanted…and she wanted him.

"I'll be back," she told him. "Just be ready."

"I'm not sure that's possible," he said.

So Cameron didn't miss the meaning in her final warning. *Good.*

Chapter Fifteen

How the hell did he go from telling himself he'd keep the intimacy and sexual tension out of his mind to sitting in Megan's SUV heading toward an unknown destination, fantasizing about peeling that dress up and over her head?

Cameron gritted his teeth and watched out the side window as his familiar town flew by. Megan may be teetering on the edge of speeding, but he wasn't about to say anything. In all honesty, he could use the distraction. He needed to focus on something other than the way she'd shown back up at his door with a wide smile, a little white dress that shifted against her thighs when she turned and those beat-up brown cowgirl boots. She'd done this on purpose. He wasn't a fool, and he knew Megan better than he knew any other woman. When she set her mind to something, she got it. Which meant he was not only fighting himself; now he'd be battling her.

He didn't stand a chance.

"Where are we going?" he asked, still not turning to look back at those tanned thighs peeking beneath the lacy edge of her dress.

"You're like a little kid." Megan turned onto a dirt road just outside the city limits. "This property is for sale and there's a cute little pond. We're having a picnic. Nobody is around, and I doubt there's even cell service here because it's nestled in the woods. It's too nice of a day to waste inside. The temperature is perfect."

Private. Woods. No cell service. Yeah, she'd definitely be the end of him. They were officially going to be alone, and Cameron knew without a doubt he wouldn't be able to keep his hands off her no matter how good his intentions may be. He was human, and every part of him wanted Megan for himself.

She pulled her SUV under a canopy of trees and killed the engine. Before he could pull on his door handle, Megan reached over the console and gripped his hand.

"No pressure, Cam." Her eyes held his; her unpainted lips called to him. "I just wanted to get away and relax. You've been tense the whole way here."

"I wouldn't say tense," he defended himself.

Megan laughed, smacked a brief kiss on his lips and patted his arm. "You're right. Not tense. Terrified. Now help me get the stuff out of the back."

Cameron had no choice but to follow her around to

the back and pull out the basket she'd hidden beneath a large red blanket. Allowing her to lead the way, Cameron had a hard time keeping his eyes off the sway of the hem of her skirt as the lace edge shifted against her skin. He knew firsthand how silky she felt, how perfectly his fingertips slid over her.

Those damn cowgirl boots were only adding to his arousal. She was so modest, so small-town girl, yet everything about her called to him on a level so primal and carnal she'd probably be terrified if she discovered just how much he craved her.

Beyond the physical pull he had toward her, Megan was the only woman who made him want more for his personal life. She was the only woman who inspired him to want to make the impossible actually work.

"I can practically hear you thinking," she called without looking back. "You're not relaxing."

Megan stopped near the edge of the pond. After giving the folded blanket a jerk, she sent it floating down over the grass. Cameron set the basket down and took a seat. She was right. The weather was rather warm for this time of year and he doubted they'd have many days like this left. Taking advantage of the time was a great idea. Now he just had to figure out how to remain in control here.

"For your information, I'm more relaxed now than I have been in weeks," he told her as he flipped the lid on the basket.

Easing down onto the blanket, Megan shifted her legs to her side and smoothed her skirt around her knees. "Liar. You've barely said a word. That tells me you're analyzing something." She pulled out two bottles of water. "Most likely you're overthinking us."

Us. They were an *us* at this point whether he wanted to admit it or not.

Megan continued to pull out items from the basket, as if discussing their confusing relationship with the surmounting tension was an everyday occurrence. Grapes, slices of bread, peanut butter, chips and cookies were all scattered around the blanket before he felt confident enough to speak.

Damn it. He was police chief, for pity's sake. He'd put up with quite a bit in his years on the force, dealt with even more before that when he'd been in the army. Yet here he was, trying to find the right words, the courage to talk to Megan as if nothing had changed.

Everything mattered where she was concerned. That's why he was so nervous about hurting her.

"Can I be honest?" he asked.

Her hand froze in the middle of smearing a generous amount of peanut butter onto a slice of bread. Her eyes lifted to his as a slow smile spread across her face.

"You must really be torn up about something. You've never asked permission to do anything and I've never known you to lie to me." She quirked an arched brow. "Have you lied to me?"

That smile held in place, and he knew she was joking. Little did she know how close she was to the truth. He had lied to her—by omission. He'd kept a secret that would most definitely crush her. And that was just the one about her brother, never mind the truth behind his feelings toward her.

"Okay," she muttered as she went back to making a sandwich. "Apparently your lack of smile or response tells me all I need to know. I never thought you'd actually lie to my face."

Cameron reached out, wrapping his hand around her slender wrist until she looked at him again. "There are things I can't tell you, Megan. You know that. Right now I wanted to talk about what's going on with us. I know you wanted me to relax, but I can't when there's so much between us that we're both trying to ignore."

"Oh, I'm not ignoring anything," she countered. "I'm giving you space to come to grips with the fact we slept together."

A soft breeze filtered through, picking up the curled ends of her hair and sending them dancing. Those silky strands had slid all over his body, he'd threaded his fingers through them, and right now he itched to touch her intimately once again.

"I handled that entire situation wrong," he told her, releasing her wrist.

She reached for another slice of bread and put it on top of the peanut butter. When she offered him the sandwich, he shook his head and started making his own.

"You were so vulnerable," he started, still recalling exactly how she'd trembled. "I was, too, for that matter. I'd hit a breaking point, though. I couldn't hold back anymore."

Megan swallowed a bite of her sandwich, reached for a bottle of water and took a drink before responding. "I don't understand why you denied either of us for so long when we wanted the same thing."

"Because in the end we *don't* want the same thing," he corrected her. "You know my stance on serious relationships, and I know you want a family. We're better off as friends, and I never meant to cross the line because now we're having a damn hard time finding our way back."

Megan plucked off a grape and popped it into her mouth. "There's no reason to turn back. Unless you think sleeping with me was a mistake."

The way her green eyes held his, the way so many questions stared back at him, Cameron found himself shaking his head. "No. That wasn't a mistake. I didn't plan on it, but no way could I call what happened a mistake."

"But you don't want it to happen again."

She couldn't be more wrong. "It can't happen again. Big difference."

With a cocky smile, she went back to her sandwich. He had no clue what that smile meant; more than likely he'd find out because he had no doubt she was plotting something. Cameron finished his sandwich and dived right into the BBQ chips, his favorite. She always kept them on hand for him at her house.

And it was all those little things that added up to make a giant impact on his life.

"So how did you know this property is for sale?" Cameron stretched his legs out in front of him, resting his hands behind his back.

Megan started putting the leftover food back into the

basket. "I have a coworker whose sister is the Realtor. She told me I could come anytime and fish or swim until the property sold. I guess the land was their parents' and now the sisters don't want it, so they're selling it and splitting the profit."

Cameron looked around at all the old oak trees, the perfectly shaped pond, complete with a small dock for fishing or jumping off. He could practically picture a large, two-story cabin-like home off in the distance on the flat stretch of land.

"Beautiful, isn't it?" she asked.

Cameron glanced back to her. "It is."

He watched as her eyes surveyed the land, saw a soft smile settle on her face. Such a look of happiness and contentment.

"You want this land, don't you?"

Blinking, she met his gaze and shrugged. "Who wouldn't? It's just another daydream, though."

He wanted her to have this, wanted her to achieve all those dreams because her entire life she'd put everyone ahead of her own needs. He knew she'd already fantasized about having a family here, kids running through the field and jumping off a dock into the pond. "Buy it," he told her. "Nothing is holding you back. Buy this land and it will be here when you're ready to build."

Megan lay on her back, her head on his thigh and her booted ankles crossed. She laced her fingers over her abdomen and stared up at the sky.

"There's so much holding me back." Her reply came on a soft sigh as she smiled. "I just want to lie here and pretend for a bit longer. I love the sound of absolute nothing. There's something so peaceful, so perfect about it. Like the world is one big happy place."

Her eyes drifted closed, and Cameron's heart broke for her. All she'd ever wanted was for everyone around her to be happy and have a peaceful life. She wasn't naive by any means, but Cameron wondered if she truly believed she could make that happen. The woman was relentless; she'd try to help everyone she knew or she'd go down swinging.

Unable to keep his hands from her another moment, he smoothed her hair away from her face, trailing his fingertip down along her shoulder. "What's holding you back from buying?" he asked.

He knew she was extremely frugal with her finances and she rarely bought anything for herself. Her house and SUV were both paid off. She wasn't a shopper like some women he knew.

Those bright green eyes focused on his. Sometimes looking at her physically hurt him, because he knew one day she'd find the one. She'd settle down and marry, probably have children. And all that happiness was exactly what he wanted for her. He just couldn't be the one to supply her needs.

"I may be moving."

Cameron's hand stilled, and the fine strands of her hair slid right out of his fingers. "You're moving?"

"I haven't decided yet."

All Cameron could do was stare. The air seemed a bit thicker as the severity of her words hit him like a punch to the stomach. He hadn't seen this coming, and it took a lot to send his shock factor gauge soaring.

"Where would you be moving?" he asked.

"Memphis."

Almost two hours away. Not terribly far, but not down the street, either, as he'd grown used to. He'd already told himself he couldn't have his job and her. Something had to give. He just hadn't been prepared to let her go so far. Damn it, he didn't want this, but she had to make her own choices.

"I was offered a position at a new facility," she told him, her tone soft as if she was afraid to go into details. "That's where I was when I went out of town."

Nodding, Cameron rested his hand at his side. "Did you like the place?"

Why did the selfish part of him want her to say she hated it? Why did he hope she would turn this opportunity down? Hadn't he just told himself he wanted to see her happy, to see all her wishes and dreams come true for once?

Yet here he was, craving her, knowing he wouldn't give in to his own desires all because he wanted her to live the life she deserved and not be tied to the stress and obligations of being with a cop.

"I did." Megan focused back on the sky as the sun took cover behind a large white cloud. "There's just so many pros and cons no matter what decision I make."

"You need to do what's best for you, not what's best for everyone else."

There, that was the right thing to say. Still, the thought of her leaving was like a vise on his heart. He didn't want her to go, but he wouldn't sway her decision unless she asked his opinion. Even then, he wouldn't tell her to stay because he selfishly couldn't stand the thought of going days or even weeks without seeing her.

She was obviously just as torn or she would've told him her decision sooner. "Have you talked to Evan about the move?"

Megan sighed. "No. On one hand, I think leaving and having him come with me would be the fresh start he needs. On the other hand, I don't know that he would come."

Cameron really wished he could tell her that most likely Evan would be in jail before long.

"Don't let Evan factor into this," he commanded, a little harsher than he'd meant to.

Megan's eyes snapped to his. "How can I not?" she asked, jerking up into a sitting position. The way she twisted to confront him had their faces within inches of each other. "He's my only family, and he needs me."

"He needs to help himself for once."

Anger flashed through her eyes. "I won't fight with you about this again. You love Eli and Drake no matter what they do, and I love Evan no matter how much he screws up. He's still my brother."

Cameron wasn't about to state the obvious, that Evan wasn't near the men Eli and Drake were. Megan knew exactly how those three men lived their lives.

Tamping down his worry and frustration, Cameron lifted his hand to her cheek. Stroking his thumb along her soft skin, he held her gaze.

"I want you to make a decision that is strictly selfish," he told her. "I want you to do whatever you want without thinking of the consequences, without thinking of who will be hurt or angry. What does Megan want?"

Without a word, she shifted away and came to her feet. Toeing off her cowgirl boots, she kept her eyes locked on to his. In a move he hadn't seen coming, she lifted the hem of her skirt and pulled the dress over her head, tossing the garment to the side. Seeing her standing before him in a simple white cotton bra and panties shouldn't have turned him on as much as it did, but every single thing about Megan had his body responding.

"What are you doing?" he asked, cursing his raspy voice.

Reaching around to unfasten her bra, Megan let the straps slide down her arms. "I'm making a selfish decision. Right now, I want to go lay at the edge of the pond and get lost in a fantasy." She met his gaze as she hooked her thumbs in her panties and pulled them down. "With you."

He'd never been one to turn away from a challenge. No matter how many warnings blared through his head, there wasn't a man alive who would turn Megan Richards away.

Even with the high, full trees, sunlight filtered through and seemed to land right on the perfect body she'd placed on display for him.

"What if someone sees us?" he asked.

Megan laughed. "Well, we're pretty secluded and nobody is around. We'll hear a car if it comes up the road. Plus I'm the only one naked, so I guess I'm the only one who should worry about being seen. Am I right?"

She quirked a brow and turned away, heading toward the deck. Cameron came to his feet and began to strip, all the while watching that soft sway of those rounded hips.

There would be no good outcome to this story. Not one. He figured he might as well enjoy every moment with her that he could, because once those warrants came through, Megan would not be throwing those sassy, sultry smiles his way any longer. She'd look at him with disdain, and the thought crushed him.

Right now, he wanted to feel her in his arms, wanted to show her he truly did love her…even if he could never say the words aloud and mean them the way she needed him to.

Chapter Sixteen

Out of all the spontaneous things she'd done in her life, not that there had been many, making love with Cameron out in the open without a care in the world had to top the list.

Come to think of it, making love with Cameron had topped any and all lists she'd ever made or ever would make.

As Megan pulled into her drive after dropping Cameron off, she realized they'd been out much later than she'd meant and she hadn't left a porch light on. The street lamp was enough for her to see, but she still hated coming home to a dark, empty house.

She didn't regret one moment of today, though. Spending the day with Cameron, not worrying about Evan or how this change in her and Cam's dynamic would affect their friendship was quite refreshing.

Speaking of refreshing, her body still tingled as she recalled how Cameron had lifted her naked body against his and walked into the water. The water had been surprisingly warm. When Cameron had knelt down, with her wrapped all around him, and made love to her as the water lapped at their waistlines, she'd fallen completely in love with him. The moment had been perfect, the man even more perfect. And she knew she'd loved him all along, but that moment, that beautiful, special moment, had opened her eyes to what was truly happening between them.

Megan pulled into the garage, grabbed the basket from the trunk and headed to the back door. Holding up her keys toward the glow from streetlights, Megan squealed when a shadow of a man stood on her back steps.

"It's just me."

Heart pounding nearly through her chest, Megan gripped her keys and the basket. "Evan, you scared me to death. Why are you out here in the dark?"

"Can I stay here? At least for tonight?"

Megan stepped forward, still unable to see him very well. "Of course you can. You're my brother."

He shrugged. "I just…I didn't know after the other night."

"Let's get inside and then we'll talk."

She opened the back door and ushered him in ahead of her. After flicking on the kitchen light and setting the basket on the dinette table, she turned to Evan.

"What happened?" she asked, examining his swollen eye and cut lip. This looked far worse than the injury from the other day. And this was the other eye because the other one still sported a fading purple bruise.

Evan sank into a wooden chair at the table. "Wrong place, wrong time. Story of my life."

She wanted to tell him he'd written his own story and it was never too late to start a new chapter, but she figured all that psychoanalyzing would only irritate him even more. It would be the equivalent of teaching a drowning person to swim. Not the time.

So, for now, she'd tend to his wounds and listen. He was here because he felt safe, and she wasn't about to run him off with all the questions swirling around in her mind or by scolding him like a warden.

"Let me get my first-aid kit."

By the time she came back, Evan had flipped the lid off the basket and was making a sandwich.

"I can make you real food if you're hungry." She sat in the chair at the head of the table and checked the supplies in the kit. "I know I have some spaghetti and a quesadilla I could heat up."

Evan shook his head. "This will be fine."

After pulling out the things she needed to fix Evan up, she turned toward him. "I only have one question."

His eyes came up to meet hers. Eyes so like hers, but they'd dimmed somewhere along the way. Perhaps the process had been slow, and that's why she hadn't noticed. Most likely the light started fading when he'd been kicked out of two schools in two years, before junior high. They'd had to move, but eventually Megan came back to her school in Stonerock because she'd missed Cameron and his brothers.

Evan's eyes definitely lost some shine on the night their parents died. Since then he'd been at a rapid decline and spiraling into a territory she feared she'd never rescue him from.

"Are you ready to get out?" she asked.

Evan reached across the space between them and gripped her hand. "Yes."

Relief flooded through her. "Are you on something now?"

She didn't need to go into details; he knew exactly what she was asking.

"No. I don't use. I only supply."

As if that made his position any better? Megan sandwiched his hand in her grip so he'd understand how much she wanted him here, how much she loved him and would support him on all levels.

"We'll get through this, Evan," she promised. "But first we need to go to the police."

"No." He jerked back, shaking his head. "I can't do that. You don't know what those guys are capable of."

Megan repressed a shudder as the memory of being held at gunpoint flashed through her mind. "I've got a pretty good idea," she told him. Easing forward, she pleaded, "Cameron can help, but you have to tell him everything."

Evan closed his eyes and sighed. "I can't right now."

Megan started to say something, but Evan opened his eyes and offered a weak smile. "Just let me get some rest tonight. Okay? Can we discuss this tomorrow?"

He was exhausted and broken. Megan's heart ached for him. But he was making progress, and she wasn't about to upset him further and risk driving him away.

The job opportunity in Memphis was weighing heavily on her mind, especially after being with Cameron again. He'd seemed stunned and speechless about her offer, but she desperately needed to know how he felt about her moving, how that would impact anything they had. At some point he was going to have to be honest with her about what he wanted.

Megan dabbed at the cut on Evan's swollen eye with a cotton ball. After applying some antibiotic ointment, she placed a small butterfly bandage on the wound and turned her attention toward his mouth.

"If we could move away, would you go?" she asked.

"Where would we go?"

Shrugging, Megan didn't want to give too much away about the job offer. "I've thought about Memphis, but I wouldn't do anything without discussing it with you."

"I like it here."

Megan nodded. "If you want to escape the mess you're in, you need to get away, and not just in theory."

A frustrated sigh escaped him. "I don't want to fight. I just want to rest."

"Fine." She wasn't going to get anywhere right now. She had to be patient. "You're more than welcome to stay. Will they come here looking for you?"

"I don't think so."

Megan finished up and started putting supplies

away. "If they come, I am calling Cameron. No arguments. Got it?"

Evan straightened in his seat. "Meg—"

She held up her hand. "No. Arguments." This was her turf, and no way in hell was it going to be penetrated by guys who were only out to cause harm.

"Fine."

He scooted away from the table, rising to his feet as he grabbed his side.

"What's wrong?" She started to reach for him, but he stepped back. "Are you hurt there, too?"

"It's nothing but some bruised ribs. I'm gonna go crash."

With that, Evan turned and headed toward the spare bedroom. Megan stared at the empty doorway, wondering how the conversation would go in the morning. Would Evan still be ready to talk about a new life or would his current fear disappear?

For now, he was safe and she wouldn't go to Cameron unless someone from Evan's circle showed up. She would do anything to keep her brother safe, and now that he was in her home, nobody would get through. She kept a gun for security in her closet. She'd never had to use it before, but she wouldn't hesitate to defend her family. No matter what.

Megan was thankful today was Sunday and she could relax. She tended to work a few hours on Saturday, so Sunday was her only full day off.

Halloween was tomorrow night. She enjoyed seeing the kids in her neighborhood all dressed up in adorable costumes. She couldn't wait until the day she got to parade her own little gremlin or witch around.

Megan had finished making breakfast an hour ago, and when Evan continued to sleep, she covered his plate and set it in the microwave. She wanted him to have a nice home-cooked meal because she doubted anyone else truly cared for him.

Her phone vibrated on the kitchen table. Glancing at the screen, she read Cameron's message.

Still coming to the cookout at my parents'?

Megan hesitated. She'd forgotten all about the cookout and bonfire, complete with s'mores, at Mac and Bev's. But she couldn't leave her brother behind to go to the St. Johns' house, and she couldn't very well take him.

Until she knew how the day unfolded, she wasn't going to respond.

By the time Evan woke, Megan had already cleaned the entire kitchen and dusted her living room. Wearing only his jeans, Evan shuffled in and sank onto the couch. His dark hair stood on end, the bruises over his face and along his right side more prominent this morning. He hadn't let her look last night and she wasn't going to coddle him today. He was a grown man, and he was here for security, not lecturing.

"Morning," he mumbled, raking a hand over his face, the stubble along his jaw and chin bristling beneath his palm. "Thought you'd be at work."

Megan leaned a hip against the back of her oversize chair and crossed her arms. "I don't work on Sunday."

"It's Sunday? I've lost track of the days." He eyed her, drawing his dark brows in. "You have plans?"

"Not really," she replied with a shrug. "You have anything you want to do?"

Evan scratched his bare chest. "I need to get my stuff sometime."

"Where is it?"

"All over. My clothes are at Spider's place. He's cool, though, so I can go there alone. I have a few things at this girl Mary's house, but she's probably sold it all by now."

As Megan listened to her brother go through his list of minute belongings scattered all around, another layer of how different their lives were slid into place. He had no stability, while she thrived on a solid foundation. He had no real friends, and she'd had Cameron and his family since grade school. Evan worried about day-to-day life, whereas Megan worried about advancing in her already successful career.

Where had she gone wrong? At some point along the way she'd missed something.

"If you have plans, go on and do them," Evan told her. "I'm going to go get my clothes and just chill here. I don't expect you to put your life on hold for me."

"I'm not putting my life on hold," she corrected him, easing around the chair. Taking a seat on the edge, she angled her body to face him fully. "Do you have a plan beyond today?"

"Not really." Wincing and grabbing his side, he

started to sit up. "I know you like details and sched-
ules, but that's not me, Meg. I'm not sure about moving, but I wouldn't mind staying here for a while if
you don't mind."

Reaching out to pat his leg, she offered a smile.
"You're always welcome here, Evan. I just can't have
the group you hang around with. I've worked hard to
get where I am and I'll do anything to help you. Consider this your home, but if anyone jeopardizes my little world, I won't back down. I'm not afraid of them."

Covering her hand with his, Evan's eyes held hers.
"You should be afraid. They're ruthless, Megan. They
don't care who they hurt, so long as they have money
and drugs. Maybe I should stay somewhere else."

"No," she answered without thinking. "I worry
when I don't see you or hear from you. You're staying
here, where I can help you."

The muscle moved in his jaw, and his eyes darted
down, then back up. "I don't even know if getting out
is possible."

"We'll make it possible," she promised.

The back door opened at the same time Cameron's
voice called out for her. "Megan?"

"Living room."

Evan's face went from worry for her to instant stone.
"You didn't respond earlier so—"

Cameron's words died as he stepped around the corner and froze in the entryway. "Evan."

The tension between these two was so thick it was
like a concrete block had been dropped into the room.

Still, she loved them both, and if they loved her, they'd just have to grow up.

"Evan needed a place to crash," she explained.

Cameron didn't take his eyes off Evan. "Looks like he was already in a crash."

"Something like that," Evan muttered.

They'd never made it a secret they weren't buddies, but still, couldn't they at least try to be civil while she was around?

Megan twisted in her seat, letting go of Evan's hand. "What's up?"

Cameron stared at Evan another few seconds before turning his attention to Megan. "I didn't hear from you earlier, so I thought I'd see if you were coming tonight."

"Actually, I probably won't."

"Megan, go," Evan told her. "Don't stay here because of me."

She glanced back to her brother, knowing he expected her to just leave him in pain. He'd just have to get used to the fact that not everyone abandoned him. Damn it, she wanted him to see that she was here no matter what and his needs came before her own.

"I really don't want to leave you alone."

"Because you don't trust me?" he asked, masking his hurt with a rough tone.

"No," she told him, purposely softening her voice. "Because I worry about you, especially after last night."

"You can come, too."

Both Evan and Megan turned to Cameron as his invitation settled in the air between them.

"You're inviting me to your family dinner?" Evan asked.

With a shrug, Cameron leaned a shoulder against the door frame. "Sure. It's no big deal, and you have to eat, too."

Megan held her breath, her eyes darting between the two men. She was beyond shocked that Cameron had invited Evan. That was the type of noble man he was. Cameron was reaching out all because he cared for her and—dare she hope—loved her.

"I don't think your family would want me there," Evan said as he came to his feet.

"They won't mind. Come with Megan if you want or don't come. No big deal. Just extending the offer."

Megan caught Cameron's gaze and mouthed "thank you" when Evan wasn't looking. Cameron's eyes held hers, a small smirk formed on his lips and Megan knew he was only doing this for her.

If she hadn't already loved him, this would've sealed the deal. He was trying. Did that mean he wanted to try more with her, as well?

"I was just heading out for a run and thought I'd swing in," Cameron stated, pushing off the frame. "Megan, I'll see you tonight."

So, he wanted to see her whether Evan came or not. When the front door closed again, Evan glanced down to where she remained seated.

"He's in love with you."

Jerking her eyes up to him, Megan laughed. "Don't be ridiculous, Evan. We've been best friends since grade school."

"The guy has always been territorial with you, but he was looking at you like... Oh, great." Evan shook his head and laughed. "Tell me you didn't fall in love with him. Come on, Meg. He's a cop."

Yeah, he was a cop. He was also perfect for her little world, amazing in bed and irreplaceable.

"Who I love or don't love is really none of your concern," she told him. "I'm not being rude, but you have your own issues to work out. Now, if you want to come with me later, that's fine. If you don't, that's fine, too. I'll be leaving at six."

Megan turned and left Evan alone. She didn't want to hear anything else about why she should or shouldn't fall in love with Cameron. The reasons were moot at this point because she'd already fallen so deep, she'd never find her way back out.

Chapter Seventeen

Keep your friends close and your enemies closer.

Cameron had always hated that saying. Having enemies so close made him twitchy and irritable.

As he glanced across the field toward Evan, who sat in a folding chair all by himself, Cameron figured if Evan was here, he wasn't getting into anything illegal. Megan could rest easy tonight.

Speaking of Megan, she'd gotten cold earlier when the sun had gone down and he'd grabbed a hoodie sweatshirt from the back of his truck. The fact she was wrapped in his shirt made him feel even more territorial. The way she all but disappeared inside the fleecy material made her seem even more adorable. How could a woman be so many things at once? Sexy, cute, intriguing, strong… Megan was all of that and much more.

She laughed at something Eli said before turning her gaze and meeting his. Instantly the air crackled. Nothing else mattered but Megan. The case should be wrapped up by tomorrow evening when the next "trade" took place. He knew all key players were supposed to be in attendance, according to their inside source.

Maybe once all of this was tied up, maybe once Evan was out of the picture and not weighing so heavily on Megan's mind and conscience, she would figure out how to seek that happiness she deserved.

Drake came to stand beside Megan, and she turned, breaking the moment. Only Eli knew of the tension between them, and Cameron doubted anyone else was picking up on the vibes he and Megan were sending out.

Cameron's gaze darted back to Evan…who was shooting death glares across the distance. Okay, maybe one more person knew something was happening between him and Megan, but Cameron didn't care what Evan's opinion was.

"You seem quiet tonight."

Cameron merely nodded as his father came up beside him. "Been a stressful time at work," Cameron replied.

"Looks to me like you have something else on your mind."

Cameron glanced to his father, who was looking straight at Megan. She excused herself, picked up a roasting stick and took it over to her brother. Cameron watched as they talked, and finally Evan came to his feet, took the stick, and he and Megan went over to the fire to roast marshmallows.

"I figured you two would figure this out eventually," his father went on.

Cameron groaned inwardly. "There's nothing to figure out, Dad. We're friends."

"Friends is a good start," Mac agreed. "Building on that only makes a stronger relationship."

Frustration slid through him. He really didn't want to get into this right now with his dad...or anybody else for that matter.

"Look, Dad—"

"Hear me out." Mac turned to face Cameron. The wrinkles around his father's eyes were more prominent as he drew his brows together. "You are overthinking things, son. Megan isn't going to wait around for you to come to your senses."

Clenching his fists at his side, Cameron nodded. "I don't expect her to. Things would be easier if she met someone and moved on."

"Easier for you?" he asked. "Because from where I'm standing, Megan only has eyes for one person. I figured you'd be smart enough to make your friendship more permanent."

"You don't get it," Cameron began, absently noting that Evan had taken a phone call.

"Get what?" Licking marshmallow off his thumb, Drake came up beside their dad.

"Nothing," Cameron stated.

"Your brother is having women problems."

Still focused on his gooey thumb, Drake laughed. "Megan giving you fits?"

What the hell? Is nothing sacred around here?

"I'm going to kill Eli," Cameron muttered.

Drake's smile widened. "He didn't tell me. Marly

did. Women just seem to be in tune with each other, but I think something happened when they all went out to Dolly's the other night."

Had Megan mentioned him to Marly and Nora? Surely she hadn't.

When he sought her out again, she was helping Willow roast a marshmallow. She fit in perfectly with his family. What would happen if he decided to take a chance? What would happen if he gave in to both of their needs and took this friendship beyond the bedroom?

"For what it's worth," Drake went on, "I think Megan is great. I always figured you guys would end up together."

Apparently every single person in his family had some creepy psychic ability because Cameron had fought the urge for years to ever make Megan more than a buddy or a pal. Unfortunately he knew firsthand just how sexy and feisty his "pal" was.

Evan rushed to Megan's side as he slid his phone back into his pocket. Just as Evan said something to her and hurried toward the front of the house, Cameron's cell vibrated in his pocket.

"Excuse me," he told his father and Drake.

Stepping away from the crowd, he pulled out the phone and read the text.

Moving day changed. 30 min.

Damn it. That's why Evan rushed out?

Cameron caught Drake's eye. "Something came up. Tell everyone—"

Drake waved him away. "Go—we know."

This family was more than used to Cameron getting called away. All three St. John brothers were in high demand in Stonerock, so it wasn't unusual for at least one of them to get called away from a family gathering.

Cameron rushed to his house to grab his work gun and Kevlar vest. Thankfully, the designated parking lot was less than ten minutes away. By the time he pulled in, he still had ten minutes to spare.

The outcome tonight was not going to be good, but right now all Cameron could focus on was doing his job. Just when he'd been about to open himself up to the possibility of a relationship with Megan, this call had come through. Was it a sign that keeping his distance was the right thing to do?

Cameron settled in with his fellow officers and FBI agents. Now all they had to do was watch and wait, and hopefully this entire ordeal would be wrapped up tonight.

He had no idea if he should be elated or terrified.

Megan had no clue where Evan had run off to and then Cameron had gotten called into work. She'd stayed behind and chatted with Nora and Marly, roasted more marshmallows than her stomach appreciated and now lay curled up in the corner of her sofa trying to read a book by the vomited light of the evil dragon.

Megan couldn't help but look at that tacky piece and laugh. Because if she didn't laugh, she'd surely cry. Some people had a beautiful art sculpture or painting as the focal point in their living rooms. Nope, Megan had this monstrosity.

Flipping through the pages of her book, Megan wanted to see when the good scenes were coming up because the current chapter was nearly putting her to sleep.

Before she could decide whether or not to give up, her cell rang. Dropping the book on the end table, she picked up her phone, not recognizing the number. Most likely a client.

"Hello?"

"Meg. I've been arrested."

Jumping to her feet, Megan started toward her bedroom to put clothes on. "What happened, Evan?"

Dread flooded her. Whatever he'd hightailed it out of the St. Johns' party for had obviously not been a good idea.

"Your boyfriend brought me in." Evan's tone was filled with disgust. "I wasn't doing anything, Meg. I need you to come get me."

Cameron arrested Evan? How the hell had the night gone from roasting marshmallows to her brother being thrown in jail?

"How much is bail?" she asked, shoving her feet into her cowgirl boots.

"I don't think they're allowing it to be set."

Megan froze. "What did you do?"

"Listen, I need you to fix this, Meg," he pleaded, near hysterics. "I don't want to be here. Call your attorney and get me out of this place."

Megan sank onto the edge of her bed. "If bail isn't an option, there's nothing I can do right now. I'll call my lawyer, but I doubt he can do anything tonight, either."

"Maybe you should tell Cameron I'm innocent," he spat, seconds before hanging up.

Defeated, angry and cold, Megan stared at the cell in her hand. In her heart she'd known this day was coming. Evan had reached out to her for help only twenty-four hours ago…obviously too late to make a difference.

Before she could allow her mind to travel into what Cameron knew about this situation, she had to call her attorney. Evan's fear had been apparent through the line. She knew from a few of her clients just how terrifying being arrested for the first time could be. No matter what the attorney's fee would be, she'd pay it and do every single thing in her power to get him away from this city where he was only staying in trouble. If he wanted to truly get away, he needed a fresh start away from the thugs he'd been with.

Hours later, Megan was still wound tight. She'd discovered there was nothing to do for Evan right now. There would be a hearing on Monday morning to decide the next step.

Megan had hung up with her attorney thirty minutes ago and couldn't go in to bed if she tried. She glanced at the book on the end table and knew that wouldn't hold her interest, either.

Heading to the hall closet, she was just about to sink to a whole new level of desperate and pull out her vacuum when her back door opened and closed.

The late hour didn't stop Cameron from letting himself in. *Great*. She wasn't sure she was ready to deal with this, with him. She was still shaking from the fact that her brother was behind bars with criminals and her best friend had arrested him.

Moving down the hall, she met Cameron just as he stepped out of the kitchen. The dark bruise beneath his eye, the cut across his other brow and his disheveled clothes stopped her in her tracks.

"What the hell happened tonight?" she cried. "Evan's arrested and you've been in a fight."

Cameron's tired eyes closed as he shook his head. "I wanted to be the one to tell you about Evan, but I knew there was no way I could finish everything up and get here before he called you."

Anger coursed through her. "You knew my brother was in trouble. Enough trouble to get arrested, didn't you?"

Slowly, his lids opened, those signature baby blues locked on her. "Yes. I've been watching him for some time now. Him and several others."

Megan felt as if someone had taken a pointy-toed shoe and kicked her straight in the stomach.

"Evan wasn't a key player," Cameron went on. "He just fell in with the wrong crowd and ended up deeper than I think he intended."

Bursts of cold shot through her system. Megan wrapped her arms around her waist and pushed past Cameron.

"So you just arrest him anyway?" she asked, moving to the living room to sink onto the sofa. "You know he's trying to break away and you still arrest him like some hardened criminal?"

Cameron rested his hands on his hips, remaining across the room. "He is a criminal, Meg. He was with the group we've been tracking for months. Evan has been running drugs."

No. This was her brother, her baby brother. She didn't want this to be his life even though he'd admitted as much to her just yesterday. He'd said he wanted to get out. She'd give anything if he would have come to her sooner; maybe they wouldn't be in this position now.

Bending forward, her arms still tight around her midsection, she wanted to just curl up and cry or scream. "You should go," she whispered, already feeling the burn of tears in her throat.

"I'm not leaving until we talk."

Of course he wasn't.

"I know you aren't happy with me right now," he started. "But you have to know I was doing my job. I can't let our relationship prevent me from keeping Stonerock safe."

A laugh erupted from her before she could prevent it. Megan sat back up and rested her elbows on her knees.

"I don't expect you to not do your job, Chief. But I never thought you'd be spying on my brother one minute and sleeping with me the next."

Okay, he deserved that. Megan needed to get all her anger out because he'd had months to deal with the fact that Evan was into illegal activities. While Megan had suspected her brother's involvement, tonight she'd been dealt some cold, hard facts—and then learned her best friend was the arresting officer.

"How could you do this to me?" she asked, her voice husky from emotion. "How could you use me like that? We've been friends so long, Cam. I trusted you with everything in my life and you just…"

Her words died in the air as she covered her face with her hands. Sobs tore through her, filling the room and slicing his heart. Cameron knew full well that right at this moment she felt she hated him, but that didn't stop him from stepping forward and squatting down in front of her.

"I didn't use you," he said, realizing how pathetic he sounded. "I couldn't tell you, Meg. I wanted to. I wanted you to know what you were in the midst of. I wanted to somehow soften the blow, but my hands were tied."

Her hands dropped to her lap as she focused her watery stare on him. Tear tracks marred her creamy skin, and Cameron knew if he attempted to reach out to wipe away the physical evidence of her pain, she would push him away.

"You mean you chose your job again over everything else. Over me."

Cameron eased up enough to sit on the edge of the coffee table, his elbows on his knees, as he fought the urge to take her hands in his. She had to get all this anger out, and he had to absorb it. There was no other way to move beyond this mess…if they even could move on.

"Wait." Megan sat up straighter, her gaze darting to the floor, then back up to his. "You were there, weren't you? The night I was with Evan and those guys showed up?"

Regret filled him, cutting off any pathetic defense he could've come up with. As if the entire lying-by-omission thing weren't enough, now he had to face the ugly truth that he'd not done a damn thing to help her.

She continued to stare at him, continued to study him as if she didn't even recognize him anymore. "Tell me you weren't there," she whispered.

Swallowing a lump of rage and remorse all rolled into one, he replied, "I can't."

He expected her to slap him, to stand up and charge from the room or start yelling and throwing things. He expected pure anger. Anger he could've dealt with.

But when she closed her eyes, unleashing a fresh set of tears as she fell back against the couch, defeated, Cameron knew he'd broken something between them. He'd broken something in her, and he had no idea how to fix it or even if their relationship was repairable.

"I want to hate you right now."

Those harsh words from such a tiny voice was the equivalent of salt to the wound…a self-inflicted wound. He had absolutely nobody to blame but himself.

Megan eased up, just enough to look him in the eye. "I want to hate you so you'll be out of my life, so I never have to see you again," she told him through tears. "But I can't because no matter how deeply you hurt me, I still love you. Damn it, Cameron, I love you more than I've ever loved anybody. I was prepared to turn down this job in Memphis for you. I was ready to fight for you, for us."

Her voice shook as she went on, swiping at the tears streaking down her cheeks. "I was ready to live with your dedication to your job. I foolishly thought you could love me just as much, but now I know I'll never be equal, never be enough."

Cameron had no clue he'd shed his own tears until he felt the trickle down his cheek. He'd never cried over a woman. Hell, he couldn't recall the last time he'd cried at all. But Megan was worth the emotion; she was worth absolutely everything.

"Stay," he pleaded. "Don't take the job. We can get through this."

"Can we?" she tossed back. "And how would we do that? You spied on my brother for who knows how long. You watched me from a distance during one of my scariest moments. I think that is enough to prove you'd never put me first, so don't preach to me about staying to make this work. I've been here for years, Cam. Years. I can't help it if you're just now ready."

Megan came to her feet, anger fueling her now if the way she swatted at the tears on her face was any indication. Cameron eased back on the table but didn't rise. He knew she needed the control, the upper hand here.

"You always said you wouldn't ever make a woman compete with your job," she went on. "But what do you think I've been doing all this time? I was with you during deployments, during the police academy and your entire law-enforcement career. You think I worried less because we were friends and not married? You think I didn't play the 'what-if' game while you were overseas or if a day or two went by that I didn't hear from you?"

Reality hit him square in the gut.

"You're right." Slowly, he got to his feet. Considering she didn't back away, he reached for her hands. "You were there for me every step of the way. I didn't see your angle until now, or maybe I was afraid to."

Megan fisted her hands beneath his. "You need to go. I'm exhausted. I've got to figure out what I can do for Evan, and I need to make arrangements for Memphis."

The last bit of hope he'd had died as he released her fists. "You're leaving."

Megan's gaze slid to the floor as she nodded, not saying a word. Conversation over.

There had never been such an emptiness, such a hollow feeling in his soul. The bond they'd honed and strengthened for years had just been severed in the span of minutes. He'd known how this would hurt her, but he hadn't expected her to erect this steel wall between them, completely shutting him out.

Cameron turned, headed toward the back door.

"Did you ever love me?" Megan's question tore through the thick tension.

Stopping, Cameron leaned a hand on the door frame to steady himself. Not only was he starting to tear up again but his knees were shaking.

"I've always loved you," he told her. "More than you could ever know."

When she said nothing in reply, Cameron headed straight out the back door. He had to keep going or he'd drop to his knees and beg her forgiveness. But Megan wasn't in the frame of mind to forgive.

He had a feeling after all he'd done to destroy their friendship and the intimacy they'd discovered, she never would be.

Chapter Eighteen

Two weeks later, Evan was still in jail. She'd been able to see him several times and each time she went her heart broke even more. He'd hinted that maybe he'd be getting out soon, but she couldn't get details from him.

After taking another picture from the wall, Megan wrapped it in bubble wrap and placed it in the box with the other fragile items. Her new job was to start in two weeks and she was moving in to her new rental within days.

The thought of leaving this house that she'd loved for so long had her reminiscing with each room she walked through, each item she boxed up. She'd yet to pack the dragon lamp because each time she passed by the hideous thing, she started tearing up once again.

In the two weeks since she'd last seen Cameron, her

emotions had been all over the place. She'd gone from angry to depressed, from crying to yelling at the empty space. Other than during his deployments, she'd never gone this long without seeing or talking to him. How could her best friend since childhood be out of her life so fast? How did she move on without the stability and support he'd always offered?

By sticking to her plans. She would move towns, make new friends and start a new life. And if Evan somehow miraculously got out, he could join her.

Of course, all of that would be in a perfect world, and she knew she lived in anything but.

Tomorrow she'd have the difficult task of telling her clients that she was leaving. She'd really formed some wonderful friendships during her time at the counseling center. Her supervisor was sorry to see her go, but understood, considering she'd been the one to recommend Megan for the position.

Before she could pull another piece of artwork from the wall, the doorbell rang. Glancing around the boxes, bubble wrap and her own state of haphazardness, Megan shrugged. She wasn't expecting company, though she'd been surprised Cameron hadn't attempted to contact her again. A piece of her was disappointed and a little more than hurt at the fact, but she'd told him to go and he was honoring her wishes. Noble until the end, that man was.

Adjusting her ratty old T-shirt and smoothing back the wayward strands that had escaped her ponytail, Megan flicked the lock and tugged on the door.

Speak of the devil.

Only he didn't look like the devil at all. He didn't even look worn and haggard as she did. Damn the man for standing on her porch looking all polished and tempting. The fall breeze kicked up, bringing his familiar scent straight to her and teasing her further.

His eyes darted behind her, no doubt taking in the chaos.

"When do you leave?" he asked, returning those baby blues to her.

Gripping the door frame, she prayed for strength, prayed to be able to hold it together while she figured out the reason for his visit.

"Next week."

He glanced down, then back up and sighed. "Can I come in? Just for a minute?"

Said the lion to its prey.

Megan stepped back, opening the old oak door even more to accommodate his broad frame. As soon as he entered, she closed the door, leaned back against it and waited while he continued to survey the room.

"I came to fill you in on Evan."

He turned to face her, and now that he was closer, she could see the worry lines etched between his brows, more prominent than ever. The dark circles beneath his eyes were evidence he'd been sleeping about as much as she had.

"What about him?" she asked, crossing her arms over her chest, resisting the urge to touch Cameron just one more time.

"I'm not supposed to tell you this, so please don't say anything. This could cost me my badge."

Megan stood up straighter. He was here as her friend, putting her above his job for once. A piece of the hard shell around her heart crumbled.

"Is he in more trouble?" she asked, fearful for the unknown.

"No." Cameron toyed with the open flap of a box on the coffee table. "He's actually going to take a plea bargain. He was offered immunity in exchange for every bit of information he knows."

Elation filled her. Megan clutched the scoop neck of her T-shirt and sucked in a deep breath. "Thank you," she whispered, unable to say anything else.

"There's more."

She tensed up at Cameron's hard stare. Whatever the "more" was apparently wasn't good news.

"He's going to go into Witness Protection first thing in the morning."

Witness Protection. The words registered but not fully at first. Then she realized what Cameron was truly telling her.

"I won't see him again?"

Shaking his head, Cameron held her gaze for a moment, then looked away as if he couldn't bear to see her. "I tried to get you in, but that power is above me. I had to fight to get the immunity. He had some stiff charges against him, but since he was a latecomer to the group, we needed the big names he could provide."

Megan nodded, hating what he was saying but knowing this was for the best. This was the only option for her brother to make a fresh start and stay safe.

"Could I write him a letter or something?" she asked. "Maybe you could get it to him?"

The muscle in Cameron's jaw jumped. "I can't."

Megan pulled in a shaky breath and pushed away from the door. Heading back to her task, something she had control over and something she could concentrate on, she pulled a picture off the wall and tore off more bubble wrap.

Methodically, she wrapped the frame, all the while coming to grips with the new level of pain that had settled deep into her chest.

"If you happen to have something that needs to be said, I could perhaps stop by and tell him before they take him away."

Cameron's generous offer hovered between them. After placing the package in the box, she closed the flaps and held her hand over the opening as she focused on Cameron.

"Tell him…just tell him I'm proud of him and I love him." Megan couldn't believe she'd never be able to tell him in person again, but if this was all she had, she was going to take it. Cameron nodded and turned to go. Megan stared at his back. Had he only come to deliver the message? Weren't they going to talk about anything or even pretend to be…what? What could they discuss at this point? She'd thrown him out weeks ago, and she hadn't extended a branch to him since.

"Cam," she called just as his hand fell to her doorknob. "Wait."

Glancing over his shoulder, he raised a brow as his eyes locked on to hers.

Gathering her strength and courage, she stepped around the coffee table and crossed the room to stand in front of him. He turned to face her, but the minuscule space between them may as well have been an ocean for all the tension that settled in the slot.

"Thank you."

Megan looked up at him, at the man she'd fallen so deeply in love with, and seriously had no clue how she would go on without Evan or Cameron in her life.

"I know Evan and I had our issues," Cameron started. "But we have one thing in common. We both love you."

Megan swallowed the tears that threatened. The last time Cameron had been here she'd cried enough to last a lifetime.

"We both want to see you happy," he went on. "Unfortunately we both had a terrible way of showing it."

Cameron started to reach out, then stopped. She glanced at his hand, hovering so close, and slid her fingers through his.

"They always say the ones you love the most can hurt you the most." The feel of his hand in hers sent a warmth spreading through her—a warmth she'd missed for two weeks. "I didn't know that to be true until recently."

Cameron's free hand slid along the side of her face. Megan tilted her head just enough to take the comfort he was offering.

"To know that you did this for Evan means everything to me," she added. "The thought of not seeing him again hurts, but it's far better than seeing him through glass. He'll have freedom and he'll be able to start over. That's all I've ever wanted for him."

"What about you?" Cameron's thumb stroked her cheek, the simple touch sending chills all over her body. "Are you going to start over?"

"That's my plan," she muttered. "It's my only option at this point."

Cameron's mouth covered hers without warning. The hungry kiss started so demandingly, Megan had no choice but to clutch at his wide shoulders. Just as she was getting used to being overtaken, Cam lightened his touch, turning the kiss into something less forceful but every bit as potent and primal.

By the time he eased away and rested his head against hers, they were both panting.

"I'm begging you, Meg. Don't leave." Both his hands framed her face; the strength of his body covered hers, and the raw words hit her straight in her heart. "I don't care if I look weak or pathetic. I'll beg you to stay. I need you so much more than you need me. You're so strong, and I know you would be just fine in Memphis. But I would not be okay here without you."

Wrapping her arms around his waist, Megan couldn't hold back any longer. The dam completely burst and tears she'd sworn never to shed in front of him again came flooding out. Cameron enveloped her, pulling her tighter against his chest as she let out all her fear, worry and uncertainty.

"I know I broke something in you with the choices I made." His hand smoothed up and down her back, comforting her. "I'll spend the rest of my life making all of that up to you. Please, please give me a chance."

"I'm scared, Cam," she murmured into his chest. "What happens when another big case comes along? What happens the next time you shut me out? What will I do when you decide the job is more important than I am or we are?"

Pulling back, Cameron looked her in the eye. "Nothing is more important than you are. Nothing. I came here expecting nothing from you, Megan. I came here to tell you about Evan, knowing full well that I could lose my job if anyone found out. I don't care. You are worth every risk, every chance I'll ever take."

Megan hiccupped as the next onslaught of tears took over. "I'm a mess," she told him, wiping the backs of her hands over her cheeks. "Look what you do to me."

His eyes focused on her. "I'm looking, and I've never seen a more beautiful woman in my life. You're it for me, Megan. I want to marry you and start a family with you. I know that's a lot to absorb right now, but just stay so we can work this out."

Megan couldn't believe what he was saying. He wanted to marry her?

"If you can't stay, if you're already committed and cannot get out of the Memphis job, or if that's really where your heart is, we can buy a place between here and there and we'll commute." Cameron kissed her lightly once more. "Just say you'll give us a chance."

"How could I refuse you?" she told him, raining kisses over his face. "How could I ever let you go?"

Cameron picked her up and started toward the hallway. "You'll never have to find out."

By the time they hit the bedroom, Megan knew she wasn't going anywhere for a long, long time.

Epilogue

"How much farther?"

Cameron squeezed Megan's hand and laughed. "Just don't move that blindfold. We're almost there."

"I think you're just driving in circles," she mumbled. "If you keep going too much farther, I'm going to get carsick. We're supposed to be on our way to our honeymoon."

They'd been married for three hours. He'd promised her a memorable wedding night, and he intended to deliver, but they weren't going far. He'd requested she keep her wedding dress on, told her it was important to him.

He glanced over, still a little choked up at the vision in white lace beside him. Her strapless gown fitted her body beautifully from her breasts to her waist with such a delicate fabric, he was afraid to touch her. In just a few short minutes she'd see why he wanted to keep her in her wedding gown. The airport could wait until tomorrow.

Tonight, he had a special surprise.

Cameron turned onto the dirt road and brought his truck to a stop just in front of the clearing. "Don't move. I'll come around to get you."

By the time he'd gotten Megan out of the truck and stood her beside him, she was looking a bit pale.

"You feeling okay?" he asked. "I thought you were joking about the carsick thing."

Megan whipped off her blindfold. "I'm not carsick— I'm pregnant," she cried.

Shock slid over him at the same time she gasped as she took in her surroundings. "What are we doing back here?" she asked.

Cameron couldn't think, couldn't speak. His gaze darted to her flat stomach beneath her vintage gown and all he could think was he was going to be a father. He and Megan were going to be parents.

With a shout, he wrapped his arms around her, picked her up and spun her in a circle, the train of her dress wrapping around his feet.

"Sickness, remember?" she yelled.

Easing her down, Cameron kissed her thoroughly. "How long have you known?" he asked when he pulled back.

"I just took a test at home this morning. I wanted to wait until after the reception to tell you, when we were alone, but then you said you had a surprise for me so I waited."

The flash of her coming down the aisle, smiling with tears in her eyes took on a whole new meaning now. She'd been radiant, beaming, a bright light coming toward him to make his life complete. She'd been there all along, and he was so thankful she hadn't given up on them.

Their ceremony had been perfect, planned by his sisters-in-law, his mother and Megan. The church had been covered in a variety of flowers, vibrant colors splashed all around. No doubt all of it was gorgeous, but he'd only had eyes for Megan. There was nothing more beautiful than seeing your best friend walk toward you, knowing you were going to start down a path that would forever bind you in love. And when she'd kissed him, he'd felt every bit of her love. And he wanted to spend the rest of his life showing her how precious she was to him.

Cameron choked back his own tears because this was the happiest day of his life. He didn't deserve all of this, but he was going to embrace every bit of it and build a family with the only woman he'd ever wanted.

"You've picked the perfect time to tell me." Laughing, Cameron held out his arms and eased the train aside with his foot. "This is it. I bought this for us to build our house on."

A wide smile spread across her face. "You're serious? You mean it?"

Seeing how happy she was made draining his entire savings completely worth it. A baby on the way, a new house and a wedding just around the holidays was a whole lot to be thankful for.

"I wanted to see you here, on our land in that dress." He reached out and stroked her cheek. "I wanted to capture this moment, this memory with you because I know it's only going to get better."

"I'm so glad I decided not to take that job in Memphis," she told him, still smiling. "How did you keep this a secret from me?"

Cameron shrugged. "It wasn't easy and I know I promised not to lie to you ever again, but I really wanted this to be a surprise."

"Oh, Cameron." Megan plastered herself against his side, wrapping her arms around his waist. "This is going to be perfect for our family. And maybe by this time next year we'll have our house done, and we can have all of your family over for the holidays. We'll have our little baby for everyone to fuss over."

Kissing the top of her head, Cameron smiled as he surveyed the land. "I think that sounds like a plan. First thing we'll move into the house will be—"

"Don't say it," she warned.

"Come on," he joked. "The lamp has to come with us."

Megan tipped her face up to his. "The only place that lamp needs to go is the Dumpster."

Squeezing her tight, Cameron rubbed her back. "Well, we can negotiate that later, but I think it would be a great piece for the nursery."

Smacking his abdomen, Megan groaned. "I will not give our child nightmares."

"You're right. It should stay in the living room. It has made quite a conversation starter."

Megan laughed, easing up on her toes to kiss his cheek. "You know I love you, but it's either me or the dragon lamp."

Turning to fully engulf her in his arms, Cameron smiled and slid his lips across hers. "You. It's always been you."

* * * * *

Don't miss a single story in the
ST. JOHNS OF STONEROCK *trilogy*
from Jules Bennett and Harlequin Special Edition!

DR. DADDY'S PERFECT CHRISTMAS
THE FIREMAN'S READY-MADE FAMILY
FROM BEST FRIEND TO BRIDE

All available now!

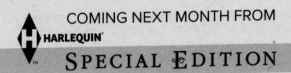

COMING NEXT MONTH FROM

HARLEQUIN®

SPECIAL EDITION

Available May 19, 2015

#2407 FORTUNE'S JUNE BRIDE
The Fortunes of Texas: Cowboy Country • by Allison Leigh
Galen Fortune Jones isn't the marrying kind...until he's roped into playing groom at the new Cowboy Country theme park in Horseback Hollow, Texas. His "bride," beautiful Aurora McElroy, piques his interest, especially when she needs a real-life fake husband. This one cowboy may have just met his match!

#2408 THE PRINCESS AND THE SINGLE DAD
Royal Babies • by Leanne Banks
Princess Sasha of Sergenia fled her dangerous home country for the principality of Chantaine. There, she assumes another identity: nanny to handsome construction specialist Gavin Sinclair's two adorable children. As the princess falls hard for the proud papa, can she form a royal family of her very own?

#2409 HER RED-CARPET ROMANCE
Matchmaking Mamas • by Marie Ferrarella
Film producer Lukas Spader needs to get his work life in order, so he hires professional organizer Yohanna Andrzejewski. She's temptingly beautiful, but Lukas must keep his eyes on his job, not his stunning new employee. As Cupid's arrow strikes them both, though, Yohanna might just fix her sexy boss's life into a happily-ever-after!

#2410 THE INSTANT FAMILY MAN
The Barlow Brothers • by Shirley Jump
Luke Barlow is happily living the single life in Stone Gap, North Carolina—until his ex's gorgeous little sister, Peyton Reynolds, shows up. She announces Luke is now the caretaker for a four-year-old daughter he never knew about. Determined to be a good dad, Luke tries to create a home for little Maddy and her aunt, one that might just be for forever...

#2411 DYLAN'S DADDY DILEMMA
The Colorado Fosters • by Tracy Madison
Chelsea Bell needs help—fast. The single mom has landed in Steamboat Springs, Colorado, and is out of money. So when dashing Dylan Foster offers her and her son, Henry, a place to stay, Chelsea's floored. Why would a complete stranger offer her help, let alone bond with her little boy? This is just the first surprise in store for one unexpected family.

#2412 FALLING FOR THE MOM-TO-BE
Home in Heartlandia • by Lynne Marshall
Ever since his wife passed away, Leif Andersen has had no time for love. Enter Marta Hoyas, a beautiful—and *pregnant!*—artist who's in town to paint a local mural. She's also living in Leif's house while she does so. The last thing Marta wants is to fall for someone who couldn't be a father to her unborn child, but Leif might just be the perfect dad-to-be.

HSECNM0515

REQUEST YOUR FREE BOOKS!
2 FREE NOVELS PLUS 2 FREE GIFTS!

⊞ HARLEQUIN®

SPECIAL EDITION

Life, Love & Family

YES! Please send me 2 FREE Harlequin® Special Edition novels and my 2 FREE gifts (gifts are worth about $10). After receiving them, if I don't wish to receive any more books, I can return the shipping statement marked "cancel." If I don't cancel, I will receive 6 brand-new novels every month and be billed just $4.74 per book in the U.S. or $5.49 per book in Canada. That's a savings of at least 12% off the cover price! It's quite a bargain! Shipping and handling is just 50¢ per book in the U.S. and 75¢ per book in Canada.* I understand that accepting the 2 free books and gifts places me under no obligation to buy anything. I can always return a shipment and cancel at any time. Even if I never buy another book, the two free books and gifts are mine to keep forever.

235/335 HDN GH3Z

Name _____
(PLEASE PRINT)

Address _____ Apt. # _____

City _____ State/Prov. _____ Zip/Postal Code _____

Signature (if under 18, a parent or guardian must sign) _____

Mail to the **Reader Service:**
IN U.S.A.: P.O. Box 1867, Buffalo, NY 14240-1867
IN CANADA: P.O. Box 609, Fort Erie, Ontario L2A 5X3

Want to try two free books from another line?
Call 1-800-873-8635 or visit www.ReaderService.com.

* Terms and prices subject to change without notice. Prices do not include applicable taxes. Sales tax applicable in N.Y. Canadian residents will be charged applicable taxes. Offer not valid in Quebec. This offer is limited to one order per household. Not valid for current subscribers to Harlequin Special Edition books. All orders subject to credit approval. Credit or debit balances in a customer's account(s) may be offset by any other outstanding balance owed by or to the customer. Please allow 4 to 6 weeks for delivery. Offer available while quantities last.

Your Privacy—The Reader Service is committed to protecting your privacy. Our Privacy Policy is available online at www.ReaderService.com or upon request from the Reader Service.

We make a portion of our mailing list available to reputable third parties that offer products we believe may interest you. If you prefer that we not exchange your name with third parties, or if you wish to clarify or modify your communication preferences, please visit us at www.ReaderService.com/consumerchoice or write to us at Reader Service Preference Service, P.O. Box 9062, Buffalo, NY 14240-9062. Include your complete name and address.

HSE15

Galen tucked the "deed" into his shirt and nudged along
his horse, Blaze, with a squeeze of his knees. He set his
white hat more firmly on his head so it wouldn't go blowing off when they made their mad dash down Main. "But
I'm definitely not looking for a career change. Ranching's
in my blood. Only thing I ever wanted to do. Amusing as
this might be for now, I'll be happy as hell to hand over
Rusty's hat to whoever they get to replace Joey." He took
in the other riders as well as Cabot and gathered his reins.
"Y'all ready?"

They nodded, and as one, they set off in a thunder of
horse hooves.

Eleven minutes later on the dot, he was pulling Aurora
into his arms after "knocking" Frank off his feet, saying "I do" to Harlan's Preacher Man and bending Aurora
low over his arm while the audience—always larger on a

Saturday—clapped and hooted.

Unfortunately for Galen, the longer he'd gone without Rusty actually kissing Lila, the more he couldn't stop thinking about it as he pressed his cheek against Aurora's, her head tucked down in his chest.

"Big crowd," he whispered. The mikes were dead and he held her a little longer than usual. Because of the lengthy applause they were getting, of course.

"Too big," she whispered back. "You going to let me up anytime soon?"

He immediately straightened, and she smiled broadly at the crowd, waving her hand as she tucked her hand through his arm and they strolled offstage.

But he could see through the smile to the frustration brewing in her blue eyes.

He waited until they were well away from the stage. "Sorry about that."

"About what?" She impatiently pushed her veil behind her back and kept looking over her shoulder as they strode through the side street. She was damn near jogging, and the beads hanging from her dress were bouncing.

"Holding the…uh…the…uh…" He yanked his string tie loose, feeling like an idiot. "You know. The embrace."

She gave him a distracted look. "What about it?"

"Holding it so long."

Don't miss
FORTUNE'S JUNE BRIDE
by Allison Leigh,
available June 2015 wherever
Harlequin® Special Edition books and ebooks are sold.

www.Harlequin.com

Love the Harlequin book you just read?

Your opinion matters.

Review this book on your favorite
book site, review site, blog or your own
social media properties and share
your opinion with other readers!

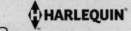